Marion Birkenbeil

Deadly Datura

Australian Crime Mystery Fiction

This is a work of fiction.
All characters in this novel are the product of the author's imagination. Real locations and events are used fictitiously without any intent to describe actual conduct.

Book idea: © Marion Birkenbeil 2023

Cover image: © Marion Birkenbeil 2023

Book typesetting: Marion Birkenbeil

Published by agreement with IngramSpark.
https://www.ingramspark.com/

Deadly Datura / Marion Birkenbeil -- 1st edition
ISBN 9780645981827 (Paperback)
ISBN 9780645981834 (EPUB)

A catalogue record for this book is available from the National Library of Australia

Note: This book is based on a part of Marion's first German novel, amended and translated by herself. Refer to page 4 for more information.

Prologue

The Kuhlmanns, a German family of four, have immigrated to Australia. They are thrilled with the beautiful Sunshine Coast, the friendly and helpful people and the fascinating wildlife. So many animals are unique to Australia! A dream comes true for Anna and Sebastian when their parents adopt a dog. Taking Susi for long walks on the dog-friendly beaches, they feel as though they were living in paradise.

But one day, two teenagers discover a woman's body in dense bushland along Stumers Creek. Everyone is shaken! A murder in their own town? What was the motive? Nobody seems to have a clue. Lizzie Kuhlmann is worried about her children who are constantly playing detective. Why won't they stop talking about the grisly crime?

Author's note to the reader:

This is a novel for everyone from 11 years onwards. Parental guidance may be required for children and teenagers as the story contains topics of drugs, depression, and a murder case.

The author

Marion Birkenbeil was born in Wuppertal, Germany in 1963. After working as a horticulturist and landscape gardener for many years, she studied landscape architecture. She immigrated to Australia in 1997. She lived with her husband in Brisbane and in Ipswich, and later they (and their dog) moved to the Sunshine Coast in Queensland. Marion is a freelance landscape architect and became a registered member of the Australian Institute of Landscape Architects in 2007.

The author and this book

The book 'Deadly Datura' derives from the third part of Marion's first German novel called 'MORD UND BRAND, FLUTEN UND SAND'. Marion has translated and amended this original German part called 'Tödliche Datura' ('Deadly Datura'), assuming full responsibility for any errors which may have inadvertently occurred. Apologies for all mistakes and any phrases that may sound odd to a native English speaker!
Marion's first novel was only meant to be a Christmas present for her mother. To her delight, this book was published by 'Shaker Media', a German publisher, in October 2013. The novel had 354 pages, many pictures of animals and landscapes, and it consisted of five complete parts. This book is no longer for sale – refer to Marion's website.

Other books

Prior to October 2023, Marion Birkenbeil has published five German books and one bilingual book. Her first English novel, a crime mystery for adults called 'Bra over Jumper – My Mum has Alzheimer's', has been published in November 2023.

Chapter 1

It was Sunday afternoon. Despite the bright sunshine, Anna had no desire to do anything at all. Lying on her bed, she stared up at the ceiling, feeling depressed. Everything came across as grey and bleak to her. And yet, she actually had no reason to feel so lousy, and she hated this emptiness that seemed to suffocate her like a dense cloud of smog. From the adjoining room, she could hear some bizarre sounds, and occasionally the voice of her brother Sebastian. He was 12 years old, about two-and-a-half years younger than Anna, and he loved computer games. He was probably playing his new one right now, alternately cheering and cursing. Lizzie, their mother, would surely have reprimanded him for his swear words! However, she was currently away, visiting a friend in town. Meanwhile, Andy, her husband, was busy in the kitchen, happily whistling along to a tune in the radio. He enjoyed cooking but always caused an indescribable mess in the kitchen.

Anna sighed. She had to do something to tear herself out of this gloominess! Mustering up her inner strength, she managed to get out of bed. She informed her dad that she was going out for a short ride, hopped onto her bicycle and pedaled away. The air was pleasantly fresh and clean after a brief rain shower at noon, and she took a deep breath. Pedaling faster and faster, she was soon feeling much better. She sped down a hill so swiftly that the wind whipped around her, tugging at her faded blue jumper that her mother had already put in the bin once. Anna had been furious and had taken it out again. It was one of her favourite clothes, no matter how worn and frayed it looked!

The street was lined with some truly majestic trees, and there wasn't much traffic at this time of day. She lived in Coolum Beach, in a hilly part of town north of Mount Coolum. An old man with a straw hat smiled at her, while his tiny dog drank greedily from a puddle on a driveway. She smiled back and turned into another street. All of a sudden, a large bird landed on her shoulder, pecking at the back of her head. Anna abruptly braked and cried out in shock. It was that beast again!

Anna had already noticed this magpie before, just recently on a walk with her best friend Barbara. Almost at the same spot, it had flown straight at a man who'd angrily waved his arms to chase it away. Barbara was born on the Sunshine Coast and knew quite a bit about the native wildlife. She'd explained to Anna, her friend from Germany, that some birds became aggressive during their breeding season. In order to defend their territory and to protect their young, they would attack dogs and people; cyclists and joggers in particular.

Barbara had suggested to attach some cable ties or pipe cleaners to her bicycle helmet. Or whatever kind of long spikes that would make it impossible for a bird to land on it. As another option, people would paint big eyes on their helmets. Would that really deter the magpies? Barbara hadn't been sure about this method. Anyway, she'd advised Anna not to act aggressively towards any magpies and other swooping birds like plovers, magpie larks, masked lapwings, and butcher birds. Otherwise, she would just encourage their defensive behaviour in the future, making matters worse. During their conversation, Anna was amused to see a woman in the same street holding up a giant palm leaf for protection. She was obviously aware of the danger!

Now, however, Anna wasn't laughing. It was scary to get attacked by a bird! Once again, the hostile magpie swooped down on her, but didn't touch her as she paused, watching it anxiously. To her relief, the magpie headed towards a street tree, where it perched on a branch and stared at her. What a meanie! Anna thought to herself. But who knows, maybe the poor bird had had some bad experiences with nasty people? Barbara had also told her that magpies were very intelligent and would remember faces. Should she smile at this particular bird now, trying to become its friend? Was it the protective father of some chicks? It seemed to be an 'early bird' as the main breeding season for the local magpies hadn't even started yet. Slowly Anna walked her bicycle up another hill, thankful for the helmet and her sunglasses. Still not trusting the bird, she proceeded cautiously until she finally dared to ride her bicycle again. She decided to follow Barbara's advice and to fix some cable ties to her helmet as soon as possible.

Back at home, delicious smells were wafting from the kitchen, and her mother and Sebastian were just setting the table in the dining room.

'Good timing! I was worried you might come too late!' Andy said to his daughter.

He carried a big bowl with a steaming vegetable dish and put it down on a wooden chopping board.

'Dad, you're caring well for your kids, too! Almost like a bird!' Anna giggled.

Over dinner, she warned her family about the swooping magpie in their neighborhood. But she also defended it, saying that it probably tried to chase away potential enemies from its eggs or chicks, and that magpies were extraordinary parents. According to Barbara, they would look after their young for up to two years.

Anna's bad mood had disappeared, and she chatted away and enjoyed the delicious dinner. She was actually eating even more than her brother who always had a ravenous appetite. Their mother smiled, content that her husband was such a good cook.

After emigrating from Germany, the Kuhlmanns lived in Western Australia for one and a half years. Then they moved to Coolum Beach in Queensland, as Andreas got the wonderful opportunity to start a new business with his Australian partner Greg, a licensed electrician. Andreas was an electrical engineer with heaps of experience in his profession, but he still needed some training and also a special skill assessment to get accreditation in Australia.

His wife Elisabeth, who preferred her former nickname 'Lieschen' or her new name 'Lizzie', was happy to be closer to her cousin's place. Paula and her Australian husband Sam were living on an acreage in the hinterland of the Sunshine Coast. Anna and Sebastian had spent their last Christmas break with Aunt Paula and Uncle Sam. Although they had never met them before, they'd instantly liked them, and they adored their two lovely dogs Missy and Lola. It had been a memorable vacation: Sebastian had sustained a concussion after a fall from a cliff. Then they'd experienced a horrifying bushfire, and later on some scary flooding. Uncle Sam had actually rescued a young girl from a wild river. What a crazy holiday!

Andreas and Lieschen were now called 'Andy' and 'Lizzie', simply because most English speakers had difficulty pronouncing their German names correctly. Although the four Kuhlmanns still felt homesick at times, missing their family and friends in Germany, they liked their new life in Australia very much. They loved the beautiful landscapes and the friendly and helpful people.

In the last few weeks, however, Lizzie noticed that her daughter sometimes seemed withdrawn and depressed. She hoped it was just a temporary phase. Was Anna sad about their move from Western Australia? Or what else was the reason for her unusual somberness? Had she perhaps fallen unhappily in love with someone? Paula had told her about Joe, the Aboriginal park ranger, whom Anna had met by chance during the summer vacation. Anna had obviously adored the young man! Well, at the age of 14, Lizzie had been madly in love with a handsome, sporty schoolmate, although she'd never really got to know him. In retrospect, it seemed absurd and silly, but she had actually daydreamed about him for two years. And yet, she'd never even spoken to him!

Sebastian was just about asking his dad about dessert, when he noticed his mother's facial expression. He grinned broadly.

'Mom, what's going on? You're looking so entranced!'

Andy chuckled.

'Yeah, the way to a woman's heart is through her stomach!'

He was very proud of his successful dinner.

Lizzie didn't admit that she had been thinking of an old, unrequited love. She simply smiled tenderly at her husband. Even after so many years of marriage, they were still smitten with each other.

Watching her parents, Anna thought that they were a great couple! They looked very youthful despite a few wrinkles around their eyes and mouths. Lizzie was blond and blue-eyed like herself, while Andy and Sebastian had dark curly hair and brown eyes. Sebastian was quite skinny and small for his age, and he often wished he were as muscular and strong as some of his new Australian friends.

Later that evening, Anna was lying awake in bed for some time. What was wrong with her? She had never had these feelings of absolute darkness and desolation in the past, but lately they overcame her from time to time, and they seemed to paralyze her – almost as if she were stuck in an invisible vice. Could it be just some sort of spring melancholy?

Chapter 2

The month of August was a lovely time in Southeast Queensland. Many native wildflowers and exotic flowers began to bloom in every color and shape imaginable, and the days were pleasantly warm when the sun was shining. Spring was fast approaching!

Sebastian would never have expected cold temperatures in the subtropics, but during June and July he was glad that his mother had insisted to bring along some warm clothes from their home country. In Germany, he had often played outside in winter, even in deep snow, and afterwards a cozy oven or central heating had quickly warmed him up. On the contrary, the homes in Queensland generally didn't have heating nor sufficient insulation. Therefore, the temperatures could sometimes be warmer outside than inside a house. Sebastian thought it was hilarious that on cold days some Australians walked around barefoot, but wore thick sweaters and beanies. However, it was mandatory to wear a uniform and proper footwear at school. At first, he had detested the uniforms! By now, though, he had gotten used to them. In general, he loved the life in Australia, regarding it as a big adventure. He was thrilled with the sea, the beautiful beaches and the wildlife. And most importantly: he had already made many new friends since their move to the Sunshine Coast in Queensland.

At times, Anna envied her brother for being such a happy, easy-going boy who didn't take everything too seriously. Nevertheless, she genuinely cared about him, and she could never be angry with him for long. Her friend Barbara was also very fond of her own younger siblings, but occasionally she got just as mad at them as Anna could be furious with Sebastian. She was in the same grade as Anna, and the two of them had hit it off right from the start. Generally a bit shy around strangers, Anna could freely speak with Barbara. While Anna was tall and slim and had natural blonde curls, Barbara was a strong, athletic girl with straight, shoulder-length dark hair and amber-colored eyes. Anna thought her friend was very beautiful. However, Barbara hated her Roman nose ever since a nasty little girl had called out to her friends:

'Look at that witch!'

One day she confessed this to Anna, who had to refrain from laughing. Anna considered her friend's nose as perfect! But she could understand her feelings perfectly. A bit embarrassed, she told her how much she disliked the numerous freckles on her own face, and was astonished to find out that Barbara regarded them as pretty. Maybe everyone disliked something about himself that others didn't notice or even admired!

The next Saturday morning, Anna was in high spirits and cycled over to Barbara's after breakfast. Thankfully, she did not have to go past the tree where that dangerous magpie had its nest! As soon as Anna arrived, Barbara opened the gate for her and whispered: 'I've already got another visitor!'

Smiling, she pointed to the garden fence. Astonished and in awe, Anna saw a giant goanna, right on top of the tall timber fence. Why did it climb up there? To hunt another animal?

'Wow, it's beautiful! But look at its long claws!' Anna said. 'Amazing how it can keep its balance!'

Carefully she stepped closer and took a photo. Sebastian would have loved to see this big lizard, also called 'Lace Monitor'. The animal seemed uncomfortable, not sure whether it should escape or pretend to be dead. The next moment, it disappeared to the other side of the fence, and the two girls went inside. The old brick house had many huge windows and glass doors with views into the garden and the adjoining forest. Anna liked the exposed timber beams and the open plan home design. As usual, it was a bit messy, but very cozy. Julie, Barbara's mother, loved to collect things, and the living room was full of books, magazines, cushions, and all sorts of paraphernalia. The dried flowers in a ceramic vase on a side table had collected some dust.

'Are you all alone?' Anna asked, surprised how quiet it was.

'No, my mum is just doing some yoga in her bedroom. And the kids are at my dad's place.'

Barbara's siblings, Lisa and Tom, were only 7 and 9 years old. Their parents Julie and Kevin were divorced but tried to remain friends. Their relationship actually improved considerably since Kevin left their house a year ago. As a result, Barbara also found life much more bearable now. Her siblings would alternate living with one of their parents, spending one week with Kevin and the other week with Julie; an arrangement that worked out quite well so far.

'By the way, I always wondered why you'd stay here all the time? Don't you get along with your father?' Anna asked.

Barbara handed her a glass of lemonade and filled one for herself.

'Well, we get along fine, but I don't want to constantly move back and forth. And my father is extremely neat and fussy! On top of that, he doesn't allow us to watch TV. All he ever wants to do is play games. I do enjoy playing ball or cards, but not all the time!'

Barbara pulled a face and took a sip of her drink. Then she grinned. 'In a way, it's nice to be without Lisa and Tom for a few days. Although I love them dearly, they can drive me nuts! And it can be annoying to be their baby-sitter! So, where is your little brother today?'

'Sebastian is playing soccer with some friends. And what shall we do? Any ideas?'

'We could take the bus to Maroochydore and go to the movies,' Barbara suggested. 'Although, um, perhaps we should rather walk to the sea and enjoy this gorgeous weather. What do you think?'

'Oh yeah, let's go to the beach!' Anna said.

Just like her brother, she found it fantastic to live in a coastal town, and Barbara's place was fairly close to the ocean. Furthermore, Anna felt she'd spent too much time indoors for the last two days. It had been raining cats and dogs. Today, the sun was shining and the sky was a magnificent blue.

'Mum, we are going for a beach walk!!' Barbara shouted, and her mother called back, 'Okay, see you later!'

Anna followed Barbara who opened the squeaky, rusty metal gate in the back garden, and they entered the adjacent forest. Hidden behind shrubs, trees and clumps of native ginger plants, there was a tiny trail that served as a shortcut to the ocean. It was quite overgrown, as hardly anyone used it or even knew about it. They had to duck under the overhanging branches of trees, climb through a tangle of climbing plants, strong Monkey Rope Vines, and find their way through lush green ferns and tall grasses. They almost had to crawl on all fours where a Paperbark tree had fallen down, and they got pretty wet and dirty. Nevertheless, they cheerfully followed the path along

Stumers Creek. It was a wide, naturalized stormwater channel that ended up at the ocean just a short distance from here. Hearing a soft splash, Anna walked a bit closer to the creek to find out what had caused it. Perhaps a fish or a water dragon? Or a snake? She couldn't see anything besides some ripples on the surface of the calm, dark water. Barbara was already far ahead now, and Anna hurried to catch up with her. The ground was slippery and muddy from all the recent rain.

'Ugh!' Anna called out, as her right shoe sank into a deep mud hole.

Barbara looked back and laughed at her. But in the next moment she let out a scream of horror, so shrill and terrified that Anna's heart seemed to stop.

'What is it?' she cried.

With a quivering hand Barbara pointed towards a certain spot on the bank.

'Over there ... is that ... a foot?' she stammered.

Anna squinted her eyes. Something did look like a brown foot. Or could it be a peculiar tree root?

'Let's check it out!' she croaked.

Barbara waited for Anna, and they went on, slowly and close together now. Both of them were gripped by fear and yet determined to find out what it was. And then they saw it clearly! There was indeed a bare foot! It was sticking out of the mud, seemingly belonging to a woman. Anna almost fainted, feeling dizzy and sick in an instant. Barbara nearly puked. Without saying a word, they turned around as if commanded to do so, and ran back as fast as they could. Anna stumbled over a tree root and almost fell over, Barbara hit her head on a branch and swore. After a few minutes, they arrived at Julie's house.

'Mum!' Barbara shouted from afar. 'You have to call the police!'

Her mother rushed out of the house. She grew pale as she listened to the confusing report by the distraught teenagers.

'What are you talking about? You found a corpse?'

She asked incredulously, reaching for her cell phone with clammy hands.

Barbara was white as a sheet of paper, while Anna's face looked somewhat greenish. They waited anxiously for the police to arrive. After a short time that felt like an eternity, a car stopped in front of the house. Two fairly young-looking men and one older woman got out and introduced themselves politely. Barbara, her mother and Anna explained everything to the police officers and quickly led them to the hidden path along the creek. Barbara went ahead, walking very fast. But close to the location of the human foot, her legs started shaking so violently that she stopped in her track. Feeling sick, she motioned to the person behind her where she had discovered the mud-encrusted foot. The police officers proceeded cautiously and asked the others to go back to the house and wait there; they would take care of everything.

This time, it seemed to Anna and Barbara that they had to wait even longer for the police. Julie paced around the living room like a tiger in a cage. She was still wearing her comfortable yoga clothes, and the timid expression in her brown eyes and the ruffled dark auburn hair made her appear very youthful and vulnerable.

Finally, one of the younger police officers returned. He was a tall, friendly looking man with blue eyes and short blond hair. He too seemed to be very distressed. In a soft, slightly hoarse voice he told them that they had found the body of a woman. She'd been shallowly buried in the mud on the riverbank.

'Why did she die?' Barbara inquired.

'I can't say!' he replied. 'We can't determine the cause of her death at this stage, but she's apparently been dead for a few days already.'

'And what will happen now?' asked Julie.

The policeman rubbed his eyes. 'First, the entire area around the body will be secured and treated like a crime scene. Some specialists will come to collect any traces of evidence, and to examine the dead person. Afterwards, she will ...' he swallowed hard, '... um, she will be transported to a mortuary and examined even more closely by forensic medical experts. And we will interview the residents in the neighborhood, especially all the ones whose back gardens border the wildlife corridor along Stumers Creek, like yours.'

Looking almost grim now, more like a strict policeman and not so much like the young guy with a baby face anymore, he asked them: 'You have not seen or heard anything suspicious in the last days?'

'No, nothing!' Julie replied.

The girls shook their heads. Only slowly did they realize that a murder had occurred.

Anna and Barbara lost all interest in doing anything else that day, and Julie took her car to drive Anna back home, just to be on the safe side. Julie was utterly shocked. A murder practically on my own doorstep! she thought to herself. In the evening, she made sure to lock all doors and windows in her house. She was tempted to phone her ex but decided against it.

Barbara curled up in bed like an infant, wrapping her arms around her knees. Over and over again, the grisly sight of the foot, sticking out of the mud, kept replaying in her mind. It had been so creepy! Good that her little siblings hadn't seen it! They all used to play in that forest since they had learned to swim, building simple huts, playing 'hide and seek' and other games. Their parents had allowed them to go into the bushland as long as they would stay close to the house and be together with at least one older, responsible kid (like Barbara) or an adult.

Barbara loved that forest! She had never been scared in it before, but now? Would her dad ever go fishing with her and her siblings in that creek again? Suddenly she missed him very much.

Anna too struggled to fall asleep that evening, tossing and turning restlessly. What had happened to that poor woman? Had she really been murdered? It definitely appeared that way because somebody had covered her body with mud. Hopefully there wasn't a serial murderer on the loose! The wildest thoughts were racing through Anna's mind. And all of a sudden, she could perfectly understand why Barbara's father did not want his children to watch TV. After all, there were so many brutal films. Even the daily news was full of violence, all over the world. But a murder so close to her best friend's home? It was hard to believe! Until now, she had been under the impression that Coolum Beach was such a peaceful, relaxed place to live. She shivered and got goosebumps.

The next morning, Anna rang Barbara straight away, asking for updates on the case. But neither she nor Julie had heard anything new yet. Only later, they got more information: The victim was Lesley Williams, a 36-year-old woman from a neighboring town. She had been poisoned, allegedly already been lying by the creek for three days. Someone had made no great effort to bury her, but simply placed her in a ditch by the bank, and covered her with the muddy earth found right there.

Due to the heavy rain and the high tide of the sea at the time, the creek water had risen sharply, temporarily inundating the corpse. Nobody had filed a missing person's report yet, and if Anna and Barbara hadn't used this overgrown trail that day, it might have taken much longer to discover the dead woman.

Chapter 3

Sebastian was upset. Yesterday, his team had lost a soccer game, and now he was having a rough time at rugby league. Once again, he had trouble with a player from the other team.

'Take it easy, mate!' his friend Jack patted him on the shoulder. 'James is already well known for playing dirty.'

'Yes, but the referee has blamed me – that's so unfair!' Sebastian complained, running his hand over his black curls.

The twelve-year-old boy was quite small and skinny for his age. Not perfect for that kind of sports! But luckily, he could run fast and change direction almost like a rabbit. However, almost everyone else on the rugby team was much stronger and taller than he was, and James from the opposing team seemed to enjoy tackling him. Just now, he had inflicted a nasty bruise on him. Sebastian was furious!

Shortly afterwards, Jack scored, gaining four additional points. Three broadly grinning guys hugged the successful player and lifted him high up in the air, and Sebastian cheered loudly. Although the conversion goal was a miss, so that they didn't get the extra two points, they won by a narrow margin.

'Yeah!' Sebastian shouted, rejoicing at their victory and forgetting his anger about James.

Only after the game, Sebastian found time to tell Jack, his best friend, in detail what Anna and Barbara had experienced the day before.

'Can you imagine that? Suddenly there was a foot sticking out of the mud! Barbara screamed like crazy when she saw that!'

'Typical girls,' Jack said contemptuously.

'Well, I would have screamed loudly too, and I bet you would have done the same!' Sebastian said defiantly.

When he got home, he was extra nice to Anna, who still seemed to be somewhat distressed. No wonder! What a shock to discover a dead woman in the bushland at Stumers Creek! Although he didn't always show it openly, Sebastian was very fond of his sister. And he knew that he could steal horses with her. He was glad that nothing had happened to her or to Barbara!

His mind was still occupied with the mysterious case when the Kuhlmanns had their dinner.

'Do you know what kind of poison was used to kill the woman?' Sebastian asked his parents curiously.

'According to the reporters, it was an overdose of sleeping pills, but forensics also found traces of a toxic plant,' Andy replied. 'Have you ever heard of the 'Angel's trumpet', the 'Datura'? Another common name is 'Devil's trumpet'. Anyway, it is an exotic garden plant with pretty flowers that are shaped like trumpets.'

Lizzie added, 'Isn't that plant called a Brugmansia? I am not sure, but I've heard about people who used some seeds to induce hallucinations and euphoria — and got terribly ill. Absolutely stupid! Why would anyone risk getting sick and disoriented, getting cramps and diarrhea, or even falling into a coma and dying?'

Andy frowned.

'I believe Daturas and Brugmansias are related and both very poisonous. I remember reading once that some teenagers experimented with one of those plants to get high. However, when they fell asleep by the sea, the tide came up and they drowned.'

'Maybe Lesley was not murdered at all? Perhaps she experienced a similar fate and drowned in the creek because she was high on drugs,' Sebastian burst out. 'It could also have been a suicide.'

'Oh, nonsense! Someone covered her body with soil, obviously trying to hide it!' Anna protested.

'But why was she killed?' Andy asked.

'And why hadn't anyone reported her missing?' Sebastian wanted to know.

'Allegedly, Lesley lived by herself, in a small house on a very large property. The neighbors apparently noticed at some point that her mailbox was overflowing with junk mail, but nobody was too concerned. Who could have imagined something so horrible?' Lizzie sighed. 'Sometimes a person passes away in his own home, and it takes days or even weeks for someone to find him. Some people are incredibly lonely, having no one to take care of them! It's so sad!'

Anna felt tears welling up in her eyes and quickly blew her nose. Although she hadn't known Lesley, she was overcome by deep sorrow. Andy gazed at his daughter, grief-stricken too. What a dreadful story! At the same time, he was relieved that nobody had attacked Anna and Barbara! What if they had met the murderer on their walk in the forest? The hair on his arms was standing up at the thought.

'But why did someone give Lesley both the sleeping pills and this deadly poison from the Angel's trumpet?' asked Sebastian. 'That's weird, isn't it?'

Anna replied:

'Well, maybe he – or she? – wanted to be absolutely sure to end her life. In any case, let's hope the killer will be arrested soon!'

Chapter 4

Sebastian was on his way to a store in Coolum Beach. 'Now I have the last laugh!' He heard a hissing voice behind him, and before he knew what was happening to him, someone kicked his bum. Four hands grabbed him roughly by the arms, forcing him to the ground. Sebastian saw James' sneering face above him, and he felt a surge of intense fear. Why did this savage dude always have it in for him? He didn't know the other kid. It was obviously a friend of James, looking equally evil and nasty. Just as Sebastian saw a fist coming towards his nose, it was snatched away at the last second. And suddenly both James and the other boy were lying on the ground. James rubbed his shoulder, his face contorted with pain, and his friend had a bloody knee. They were perplexed!

'Hey, do you still remember me?' a huge guy asked Sebastian cheerfully.

That was Peter, Mike's older brother, who had quickly intervened! Mike was one of the new friends of Anna and Sebastian who they'd met during their last summer vacation. They lived close to their relatives, Aunt Paula and Uncle Sam, in the hinterland of the Sunshine Coast. Peter was a muscular young man and over two meters tall, a truly impressive guy!

'Let's go and I'll buy you an ice-cream!' He spoke kindly to Sebastian, who was still stunned. The other boys took off, but not before giving Sebastian another threatening glare.

'Thanks, Peter, I am so glad you helped me!' Sebastian said as they walked towards the ice cream shop. 'No way I could have dealt with these two bastards on my own! For whatever reason, James never liked me, and yesterday we already had a run-in at a rugby game.' Sebastian smiled lopsidedly. 'So, what are you doing here in this part of the world?'

'I have a few days off. I had to do something in Maroochydore, and now I am going to visit some friends,' his protector replied. 'By the way, Mike, Kylie, Scott and Susan came along as well. I just dropped them off at the beach.'

'Awesome! I'll let Anna know straight away!'

Grinning in his usual cheeky way, Sebastian phoned his sister while Peter bought two ice cream cones. Anna was thrilled. She and her brother hadn't seen their friends for a long time, and she would love to meet them. She decided to ride her bicycle to Tickle Park, which was located near the main beach, and she asked Sebastian to wait for her there. Once she arrived, Peter briefly said hello to her and then hurried off. Anna and Sebastian were stepping down to the beach, looking for their friends from the long set of aluminium and timber stairs, when Scott spotted them. He jumped up and raced towards them.

'Hi! We were just talking about you, wondering if you were at home today.' Scott shook hands with Sebastian and gave Anna a quick hug – although he was still wet from swimming.

Anna blushed a little. He wasn't exactly what she'd call handsome, as he was quite skinny and gangly, but she liked his special charm. He had a dazzling smile and beautiful, sparkling blue eyes.

'Then why didn't you visit us?' Sebastian asked indignantly. 'At least you could've called us!'

Now Scott blushed and wasn't quite sure how to respond to that. Luckily, his little sister Susan came to his rescue. She ran up to them in a brightly colored bathing suit, patted Sebastian happily on the shoulder and beamed at Anna.

'Hi, you two! Kylie and Mike wanted to go surfing, and therefore Peter has dropped us off here.'

She waved to her friends out in the ocean, who were lying on their surfboards, waiting to catch a big wave.

Susan shuddered. 'Brr, I am freezing cold! Sebastian, let's race! All the way to the fisherman over there, okay?'

And she and Sebastian started to run.

Scott smiled at Anna and pointed to the edge of the dunes.

'Our stuff is over there, let's sit down for a while.'

They sat down on a huge beach towel and looked out over the open sea. It had a beautiful, clear, turquoise-blue color. The gently rippling waves were not really suitable for surfing today but perfect for swimming. Anna glanced at Scott and admired his almost naked, slender figure and his smooth skin.

'You have pretty freckles,' said Scott after the initial, somewhat awkward silence. 'Be careful not to get a sunburn, you have such fair skin!' He put his cap on her head and grinned broadly.

At that moment a young dog came by, briefly sniffed at Anna's bag and Scott's T-shirt, and then it shot away like lightning, with the shirt in its mouth.

'Hey, stop!' Scott yelled, running after the little dog.

Of course, that only increased the dog's fun, making it run away even faster. Its owner and Anna joined the chase, but it took a while to catch the puppy and to retrieve the T-shirt. Thankfully it didn't rip!

The dog's owner nevertheless felt very embarrassed.

'I had my little Rusty on the leash, but somehow he got free and took off!' he apologized.

Although they were slightly out of breath after the chase, Anna and Scott decided to go for a walk along the beach.

'Do you like dogs?' Anna asked, enjoying the cool water at her bare feet and watching some other dogs playing in the distance.

'Oh yes, dogs and elephants are my favorite animals!' Scott replied.

'Sebastian and I always wanted to have a dog, but we still have to convince our parents to get one,' said Anna. 'My mother is a bit scared of certain dogs, such as German shepherds and huskies. But she really likes the two dogs of Aunt Paula and Uncle Sam, although they are also quite big. Well, you've seen them. They are cute, hey?'

The initial tension between them was now gone, and they chatted happily until they returned and joined up with the others. Unfortunately, the four friends from the hinterland couldn't stay in Coolum Beach very long as Peter would pick them up again soon.

Anna had felt a delightful tingling sensation sitting so close to Scott, and she hoped to see him more often in the future. He kissed her goodbye on the cheek, and for a long time afterwards she felt as if she could still feel his warm lips on her skin. She pushed her bicycle back home while Sebastian walked beside her, talking non-stop. He was such a chatterbox! She only heard about half of what he was saying, because she was still thinking about Scott. Their unexpected meeting had been so wonderful!

'Hi, Mum, we are back!' Sebastian called out when he and his sister stepped into their living room.

Both of them spotted it at once: there was a dog under the table! Their mother was just cleaning a book shelf and waved at them with a dust cloth.

'Whose dog is that?' asked Sebastian, squatting down to get a better look at it.

'Is it a stray dog? Did you find it on the street?' Anna inquired.

Lizzie grinned mischievously.

'This is Susi, our foster dog! She needs a new home temporarily, as her owner has become very ill and can't take care of her.'

The dog was black, with some white spots on its chest and paws, and beautiful brown eyes. It was looking warily at the kids.

'Hey, Susi, come here!' Sebastian coaxed her, and she trotted towards him, even though she seemed slightly nervous.

'She's a mix of a Labrador and a Border-Collie. Still very young, and quite timid towards strangers' explained Lizzie.

'Hi sweetie! You're so pretty!' Anna said, and both children caressed the dog lovingly.

That evening, they had roasted chicken, fried potatoes and salad for dinner. While everyone was busy clearing away the dishes, Susi jumped up and grabbed the leftover chicken in the blink of an eye. The plate fell down, crashed on the floor, and at the same moment Lizzie screamed 'No!' so loudly that the dog dropped the meat, peed from fright and crept under the table with its tail between its legs. What a mess!

Later on, they laughed about this incident, and Susi never stole anything from the table again, even though she was always as hungry as a wolf, gobbling down her food way too fast. The Kuhlmanns went on many hikes with Susi. To their surprise, Susi couldn't swim and was afraid of deep water! Sebastian was keen to teach her. Whenever they came to a creek or a calm river, he threw a ball into the water, very close to the bank. At first, Susi hesitantly walked around in the shallow water, looking anxiously at Sebastian. Gradually, she ventured into deeper water to retrieve the ball, clumsily paddling with her legs and splashing around wildly. Over time, however, she became braver, and Sebastian would throw the ball further and further into the river. Bit by bit Susi turned into a great swimmer! The hotter the temperatures got, the more often Susi could be found in the water. On the beach, she loved to cool down in the rocky pools hollowed out by the sea. Unfortunately, she also enjoyed taking a bath in all sorts of dirty puddles in other areas. Sometimes she looked like a muddy pig!

About three weeks later, Lizzie got a phone call from Susi's owner. He explained in a faltering voice that he was still very sick. On top of that, he had to move out of his rental property, and his new landlord would not allow any pets. So, he asked them if they wanted to adopt Susi. Although Anna and Sebastian felt genuinely sorry for the man, they were as happy as Larry to keep Susi. They danced around madly, and Lizzie and Andy beamed. Even they could hardly imagine their life without this dog. All of them loved her deeply!

Anna and Sebastian took turns walking the dog before going to school. They got to meet many other locals with their dogs, and often they saw a woman pushing a stroller with a tiny dog in it. They found out that the dog tired very quickly because of an incurable disease. As soon as its energy was depleted, the nice lady put it into the stroller. Another old lady named Ina was always outside her front door, ready to chat. She seemed to know every Tom, Dick and Harry, and she always had something to talk about. Anna liked her, even though she was very nosy and somewhat tactless. But Susi was afraid of Ina, and whenever she tried to pat her, she jumped back a meter. That woman was too pushy and too loud for her!

'Hey, Anna, I've heard that you found a dead body,' Ina called out to her one early morning.

The sun had just risen, sending a warm glow over the front garden and Ina's pale, narrow face.

'Well, my friend Barbara discovered it,' Anna replied bashfully. She spoke in a soft voice, fearing that their chat would wake up all the neighbours.

Ina didn't seem to share her concerns as she was talking loudly: 'My sister was actually acquainted with that poor woman who got killed! She worked as a saleswoman in the same small grocery store, imagine that! Lesley was always very friendly, and the customers loved her. Who would've wanted to kill her? It's hard to believe, she was such a lovely woman!' Ina babbled on, looking sad. Finally, she said: 'And I never expected that I'd live to see the day that someone is murdered in this sleepy town! Great that you have a dog to protect you.'

Neither Anna nor Sebastian regarded Susi as a guard dog. However, one morning Sebastian encountered James in a deserted street, and his enemy kept his distance. Was he afraid of Susi?

Sometimes the entire Kuhlmann family went to the beach, which Susi always enjoyed the most. She was also extremely happy when she met Daisy, a little white fluffy Terrier mix. They were best pals! Daisy was only one year old, and she loved to run around joyfully with her two-year-old friend Susi.

Anna kept thinking back to the time with Scott, and she missed him. It was unfortunate that he lived so far away! Although it only took about 45 minutes to drive to his place by car, it was impossible to get there using public transportation. Her memory of Joe, the good-looking park ranger she had a crush on before, during their last summer vacation, had long faded. But Scott sparked a flood of emotions within her. She wondered what he thought of her. And when would she see him   again?

Chapter 5

Ever since her gruesome discovery, Barbara avoided the forest behind their back garden, not daring to enter it. However, one day when Anna came to visit with her dog, they decided to take the shortcut to the ocean once again. After all, they'd always liked the secret path behind the gardens. Furthermore, the access to this bushland would be limited in the near future. Two lots adjoining to the forest, that had been empty for a long time, were up for sale. Soon, somebody would build houses there, and probably fence off the properties. And then they would not be able to walk from here to the beach anymore.

It was a bright, sunny day. Both Anna and Barbara were feeling queasy and had clammy hands as they hiked along Stumers Creek. This time Anna went ahead, and Barbara got a fright when her friend suddenly stopped, shouting, 'Look at that!'

'What is it?'

'A termite nest!'

Anna pointed to a huge termite nest high up on the side of a dead tree. It looked like a big bowl.

'Wow, that's huge!' Barbara was smiling now, relieved that Anna hadn't found another dead body!

Shortly afterwards they came to the spot where the foot had been sticking out of the mud. By now, there was no evidence whatsoever of the tragedy that had happened here. Susi kept jumping into the creek to cool down, plunging around joyfully. To Barbara's dismay, she shook the water out of her fur every time she was right next to the girls.

Barbara squealed. 'Oh no! Bah! Anna, you should teach your dog to shake somewhere else! Hey, look! Susi has something in her mouth! What's that?'

'Susi, give!' Anna commanded, and Susi obediently put a soaked, brown leather watch band in her hand. Anna felt a shiver running down her spine.

'Oh boy, that might have been Lesley's!'

'Nah, it's too big, it must have belonged to a man!' Barbara said. And then she called out, 'It could be the watch of the murderer! Is it still working?'

Anna took a closer look.

'It stopped at 7:30. Oh, and there's a date here too. That must be the date when the woman was killed! And look here, the clasp on the band is broken. Maybe they had a fight and the woman tried to defend herself.'

'I can't believe it!' Barbara exclaimed excitedly.

Instead of going to the beach as planned, they went to the police station to turn in their find.

Julie was shocked when her daughter told her about the broken watch band, sharing her suspicion that it might be connected to the murder case. Julie didn't even want to think about that terrible story anymore. Moreover, a horrible idea popped into her mind. She had recently noticed a new watch on the wrist of her husband, as he came to pick up Lisa and Tom. Should she ask him about it on his next visit? There was no way he could have had anything to do with the dead woman! But still, that tiny bit of doubt took hold and kept nagging at her.

* * *

In Australia, many people are passionate about racing, regardless of the type of race. There are not only horse and dog races, but also crab races on the beach, and even races with cockroaches at parties. This Saturday, a toad race was scheduled to take place on the lawn in Tickle Park. Anna and Sebastian had never seen one before and were curious, although they didn't particularly like cane toads. As Sebastian had insisted on finishing a computer game first, they arrived a little late at the park. The race was already in full swing, and a crowd had gathered around a marked area. They heard whistling, shouting and laughter.

'Run quicker, Fast Julia!'

A boy cheered on his cane toad which had the number 4 painted on its back.

'Wise Harry, don't be so slow!' shouted a bystander. 'I've bet 5 dollars on you!'

The warty cane toads were surprisingly fast, in spite of their rather ungainly and cumbersome appearance. One cane toad escaped and had to be caught. The owner grumbled, putting it in a cage and saying: 'Naughty Larry!'

'Hooray, well done, Swift Vicki!' some people now cheered.

'This is hilarious!' Sebastian grinned. 'But I prefer frogs over these poisonous cane toads!'

Inwardly he had mixed feelings about this race, feeling sorry for all pets kept in cages. Cane toads were regarded as a pest in Australia. They had been introduced from another country, posing a great danger to the native wildlife. And to pets as well! Some predators had learned to avoid the venom glands of the toads, but many others were not so lucky. Sebastian had heard about birds, dogs and snakes that had died after eating a cane toad. Nevertheless, Sebastian hated any cruelty against animals, even if they were poisonous. Just recently he had seen a whole family hitting at cane toads with golf clubs, having fun. Sebastian had been very upset about this brutal method of killing them, and he'd almost started a fight with the father of the kids.

After the race, Anna and Sebastian walked home, chatting away. They were almost at home when they noticed a boy sitting at the side of the road, holding his head. A bicycle was lying beside him, and a large dog barked excitedly at them.

'Oh no, he's bleeding heavily!' Anna cried out.

She was startled and didn't know what to do. Blood streamed from a wound just above the boy's right eye. What could they use to stop the blood? Should she rip off a part of her T-shirt? Sebastian reacted instinctively, knocking on the door of the next house.

'Help, help!' he shouted as loudly as he could.

A young man rushed out, looked at the boy and ran back inside. He returned in no time at all and administered first aid. He wrapped a bandage around the wound, and then he gave Anna an ice pack to hold against the boy's head. Meanwhile, Sebastian was looking after the dog, taking its leash and talking to it in a calm voice. By now, Sebastian had realized that the injured boy was the one who had recently tried to beat him up, together with James. Now he didn't look hostile at all but very miserable and dazed. The helpful man offered to park the slightly damaged bicycle in his garage and to take the boy to the doctor's. He suggested that Anna and Sebastian should take care of his dog in the mean-time. Luckily, it was a friendly dog, and so they agreed.

About an hour later, the boy came to pick up his dog, accompanied by his mother. His wound had been stitched and he had a fresh bandage on his head. He also had his arm in a sling, and he told them that his arm was broken. His name was Bob.

Somewhat embarrassed, he mumbled, 'Thanks for helping me!'

His mother added: 'Thanks so much, that was really kind of you!'

'What has actually happened to you?' Sebastian asked Bob.

'Um, I was riding my bike with my dog on the leash, and Lucas suddenly wanted to chase a cat and made a big jump. And that's when I lost my balance and fell on my head.'

Lucas licked his hand as if to apologize.

Barbara had also been to the cane toad race with her siblings and Kevin, their father, without spotting Anna and Sebastian in the big crowd of spectators. Just for fun, Kevin had placed a bet with some friends, betting on Swift Vicki. And he won $20! He used the money to buy some ice cream for his children. When he dropped them off at their house, he was just about to leave when his ex-wife Julie ran up to him.

'Hi Kevin, come in! Have a slice of that cherry chocolate cake that you'd always loved!'

'Oh, okay, why not?' Kevin was astonished about the invitation.

But he couldn't resist the delicious smell of the cake and followed her into the house. Barbara was surprised too, inwardly hoping that her parents would reconcile. While they were eating, Julie peeked at Kevin's new wristwatch. Once again, she wondered if she should say anything. What the heck! she thought and decided to go ahead.

'Kevin, can you believe it? Anna's dog has found a watch, down by the creek! It probably belongs to the murderer!' she said, doing her best to sound casual.

Kevin almost choked on his hot coffee.

'How would you know whose watch it might be?' he croaked hoarsely.

Instantly, he was concerned about his family again, being so close to the scene of a terrible crime.

'Well, the watch stopped on the very day the poor woman died,' Julie replied, wondering why Kevin was acting so strangely.

Barbara picked up the last few crumbs of the cake on her plate.

'It was a bit of an unusual leather watch band. Actually, you used to have a similar looking one, Dad! Do you still have it?'

This time it was Julie who almost choked. Why did children always have to be so direct?

Kevin glanced at his new watch.

'No, I threw it out. The glass was all scratched up and the band didn't look good anymore. Besides, I always wanted to get a waterproof watch that I could go swimming with.'

'Had you ever met Lesley?' Barbara asked her parents. 'Anna told me that she'd been a saleswoman in that little shop in Peregian Beach.'

'Yeah, I've seen her a couple of times there,' Kevin said. 'She was always very nice, unlike that old cheapskate who owns the shop. He's a mean and unfriendly guy. He once caught a woman trying to steal something in his shop, and he just snatched her handbag from her and threw it up on the roof!'

Barbara laughed merrily.

'And what happened then?' her little siblings asked in unison.

'The woman screamed bloody murder, and finally the nice saleswoman fetched a ladder so that the thief could retrieve her handbag from the roof. But she had to climb up herself, and she is said to have been bright red in the face, probably from sheer anger and shame. Some people were already standing around and watching her. They were quite amused! Some even took photos of her – pretty embarrassing, hey?'

'Well, it seems like she got a good lesson there! Hopefully she never stole anything ever again!' Julie said.

Glancing at her ex-husband, she asked herself whether he could be capable of murder. At the same time, she was ashamed of even having such a disgusting thought! But the next moment it occurred to her that Kevin also had an 'Angel's trumpet' in his garden. Once she had admired the pink, beautiful flowers of this exotic plant when she was there to drop the children off. Although, hadn't he called that plant something else? She couldn't remember the exact botanical name, but it had started with a 'B' and ended with something like 'mansion'.

Barbara was also wondering about the owner of the watch. Who had gone for a walk along the creek? Few people knew about the narrow path in the bushland. Had her neighbors seen or heard anything out of the ordinary? Surely the police had already spoken with everyone. And her mother had also talked about the corpse with many of their neighbours. But nobody seemed to know anything. Nobody even had a clue about the motive for the homicide.

After dinner, Barbara went into the garden and could hardly believe her eyes – at the same place where she had recently seen the big lizard, she now spotted a pretty tree snake. Her garden fence seemed to be a popular spot for native animals!

'Lisa and Tom, come and have a look!' she shouted to her siblings.

Chapter 6

The sun had already set and darkness had fallen, but Kevin didn't switch on the lights in his living room yet. Motionless he was sitting on his sofa, once again musing about the murder. Why had Lesley been killed? She seemed like such a nice person! Since he had moved away from Julie, he had occasionally gone shopping in the small store, on the way back home from work. Who could have hated Lesley so much? And why had anyone gone through the trouble to transport her to the creek, and then not bothered to bury her body a bit deeper? Or had she been murdered right there? Next to the creek where she was found?

What a gruesome story – and such a terrible experience for Barbara and Anna! He was worried sick about Julie, Tom and Lisa. Should he move back to them just for a while? Until the killer was arrested? No, sharing the house with his ex-wife would probably not work out well. It could just lead to a new string of arguments! Kevin sighed, switched on the lights and went into the kitchen to prepare a simple dinner for himself.

Later in the evening, he spent some time on his laptop, searching for information about Daturas and Brugmansias. The intoxication and possible side effects of drugs derived from these poisonous plants sounded extremely unpleasant, and there was a very thin line between hallucination and death by heart failure. Why would anyone take such a risk? It was far too dangerous! And outright stupid to experiment with toxic chemicals, especially for an inexperienced layman!

Kevin thought of his three children. He loved them dearly, and he hoped they would never attempt to use a toxic plant as a hallucinogen. Maybe it would be best to get rid of the Brugmansia hybrid in his own garden! The former owner of his property had planted this beautiful exotic shrub in the back garden. Its large pendent flowers were quite impressive! Kevin was not sure about the exact botanical name, but he believed this tall shrub shared the same common name with another toxic plant called Datura, namely 'Angel's trumpet'. But should he really eradicate such a pretty shrub? He dismissed that idea and decided that he'd rather inform his kids about the possible danger of certain plants. After all, there were thousands of poisonous plant species around the world! It would be madness to get rid of them all! In fact, many of them were very useful as medicines – if you understood how to use the substances in the correct way.

Kevin kept on reading. He discovered that many native plants in Australia were toxic to animals and humans as well. Some plants could be very dangerous, even deadly, others could cause allergic reactions or dermatitis. Just touching certain plant species could trigger itchiness, rashes or weepy blisters. Some plants had poisonous prickles or contained an irritating sap, possibly endangering the eyes.

He was glad that his children were no longer babies who'd love to put all sorts of things into their mouths! Nevertheless, it would be good to learn more about plants, both in his own garden and in natural environments! His ex-wife Julie was quite interested in bush tucker food. She actually had a fairly good knowledge about edible plants. But even she had once been careless and got tempted to taste some unfamiliar nuts – until her brother warned her off, as those nuts were toxic when eaten raw.

Kevin's thoughts returned to Lesley. Had she deliberately experimented with the deadly Angel's trumpet, perhaps together with a friend? Maybe it had just been an accident, causing her friend to panic, and to bury her after her sudden death? He was keen to find out more!

The following day, Kevin went to the small grocery store where Lesley had worked. A young saleswoman greeted him warmly. The owner of the shop was busy in the back, sorting and labeling new goods. Kevin pondered whether he should strike up a conversation with the staff. How could he bring up the topic of the murdered woman? Should he simply ask about Lesley, pretending not to know about her death? Still indecisively, he walked down the aisles, checked out the products and put some bananas, a cauliflower, milk and cheese in a basket.

'Excuse me, where's the mustard?' he asked the saleswoman.

She guided him to the right aisle and showed him the rack with the mustard jars, smiling friendly as he chose his favourite Dijon mustard and some sweet mustard pickles.

'Have you been working in this shop for a long time?' asked Kevin. 'I'd never seen you before.'

'No, I only moved here from North Queensland about a month ago. I was very lucky to get this job right away. Fred…,' she nodded towards the old man, 'told me about the former employee. That was a terrible tragedy!'

At that moment, Fred came towards them, and she quickly returned to the cash register. Kevin was pretty disappointed that he hadn't obtained any information about Lesley. But what exactly had he expected?

Chapter 7

Anna's father was at home, studying some technical drawings that were spread out across his large desk. He had just been assigned a new project: a design for the electrical wiring of a proposed apartment building in a neighboring town. Anna peered curiously over his shoulder as he examined the blueprints of the planned buildings. When she saw the Real Property Description in the title block of the plans, she gasped. It was the address of the killed woman! Ina had told her Lesley's address. Anna remembered it very well, as she had been amused at the street name:

Number 17 Frogmouth Street, Peregian Beach.

'Dad, this is Lesley's property!' she said excitedly.

'What?' Andy frowned. 'Nah, according to these plans, the owner is a man. He intends to tear down the old two-story house and build an apartment building. Unfortunately, this is our new world, with more concrete, more streets, ever smaller gardens, and high-density housing. The construction companies are happy about it. I'm just glad that it's not allowed everywhere to subdivide large properties and to build high-rise buildings or townhouses. And I surely love my own big garden!'

As if responding to his words, a group of kookaburras started to sing loudly.

'These birds always sound funny, don't they?' Anna said with a smile.

The concert continued for a while. The German name for them was 'Lachender Hans', the common English name was 'Laughing Kookaburra' or 'Laughing Jackass', all of them appropriate names as you couldn't help but grin when you heard the amazing laughter of these pretty birds.

The next day, Anna, Sebastian and Barbara decided to visit Lesley's former home at the weekend, determined not to tell anybody else. Their parents would probably get upset for no reason if they knew about their intention to sneak around a bit. On Saturday afternoon, they met at Barbara's place and cycled together to the property in Peregian Beach. It was a distance of about 5 kilometers, and the route was pretty flat. The sky was overcast, but the sun broke through the clouds just when they arrived at their destination. The whole property was secured with a construction fence. They parked their bicycles on the verge and looked around curiously. Most of Lesley's old house had already been demolished and several big trees had been cut down. Only the huge stumps hadn't been removed yet, and one tree was lying beside a shed, with its giant root system exposed. A crow croaked hoarsely somewhere in the distance, contributing to the eerie atmosphere. Anna felt an icy shiver running down her spine.

Ignoring the signage 'No unauthorised access', the teenagers slipped through a gate that a worker had evidently left open. Everything looked very desolate and bleak. Dirt and plant waste were dumped in one corner, old bricks in another one, and wooden beams and parts of the roof were piled up somewhere else. In two large dumpsters, they saw all kinds of rubbish, including broken glass and tiles, some old carpets, a mattress and furniture. They carefully walked around some debris to explore what was left of the house. All three of them felt a little creeped out, fully aware that the former owner of the house had been murdered.

'What about Lesley's relatives? You'd think they would inherit the property,' Barbara said in a muted tone. 'Didn't she have any children or siblings?'

Anna shrugged her shoulders. 'I guess not!'

'Maybe she got knocked off at home,' Sebastian whispered.

Both Anna and Barbara looked at him, appalled. They had never considered that possibility, automatically assuming that the crime had been committed at the creek. There wasn't much left of the top floor of the house, and rubble was lying around everywhere. In one room on the lower floor, however, they found an antique looking cupboard and a huge wooden table.

'How strange that nobody took this beautiful furniture,' Anna remarked, touching the cupboard slightly, almost reverently. 'This must have been the living room.'

'Look, there's a framed picture hanging on the wall!' Sebastian called to them from another room. 'Maybe Lesley drew it herself.'

Anna studied it carefully. 'That girl looks awfully sad. Who do you think it could be?'

'And here is another drawing of an ancient looking couple,' Barbara exclaimed, carefully wiping the dust off to make it easier to see. 'Weird! The woman's hand is much too big and the man's too small!'

'Maybe it's a picture of her parents?' Sebastian wondered.

'Yeah, who knows. Come on, let's get out of here!' said Barbara.

Just like Anna, she was feeling more and more uncomfortable in this place. Sebastian would have liked to snoop around a bit more, but he followed the girls and left the construction site. A few Australian white ibises flew away from one of the dumpsters, startling him.

Barbara laughed when she saw his anxious face.

'They are scavengers, and some people call them 'bin chickens' or 'dump ducks' as they often search for food in rubbish dumps!'

On their way home, enormous clouds rolled in, followed by a heavy downpour, and they got soaking wet. Somehow Barbara was thankful for the rain. She had the feeling it not only washed off the dust from her skin but also removed all sinister thoughts from her mind. She felt so sorry for the murdered woman even though she hadn't known her!

Chapter 8

As soon as they arrived home the rain stopped. Taking a hot shower, Anna suddenly had an idea. She could hardly wait to tell her family!

'Listen up, I know who the murderer is!' she shouted triumphantly when they had their dinner.

'Who is it?' asked Sebastian, with his mouth full.

'It must be the builder!'

'What? You have a wild imagination!' her father said.

But Anna was not going to be dissuaded.

'Well, it's quite clear to me. The man wanted to buy Lesley's property so that he'd be able to construct a multi-residential development there, and to make heaps of money. But since Lesley didn't want to sell her house, he came up with another plan. He made her a special tea using the Datura plant to intoxicate her so that she would be willing to do so. If she were high as a kite, perhaps she would sign a sales contract? And later, he hoped, she wouldn't remember exactly what had happened. But when this plan didn't work out, he quickly mixed a lot of sleeping pills into a drink and killed her that way. We've read that the plant drug is supposed to make you very thirsty.

So, it certainly would have been easy to make her drink the toxic tea. And after her death, he managed to snap up the property because she had no relatives!'

Sebastian was instantly hooked on her idea, but her parents had their doubts. Lizzie snorted in disgust, and Andy shook his head.

'I'd already told you before: better be careful with your malicious and unfounded allegations!' he admonished his children sternly.

A few days later, Andy had a meeting with the boss of the construction company. They discussed the plans for the electrical installation of the proposed buildings in Frogmouth Street. Back at home, he told his family how nice Ray had been.

'No way this man could be a murderer,' he said to Anna. 'Ray is a chubby, laid-back and funny guy who wouldn't hurt a fly! We even talked briefly about Lesley. He was acquainted with her and said that she was a very likable woman, although she occasionally suffered from depression and was rather quiet and reserved in general. She lost her husband in a car accident, just a few years after their wedding, and she probably never got over it.'

'The poor woman!' Lizzie exclaimed. 'And now she's been murdered! But why? And by whom?'

Barbara's mother Julie also asked herself this question over and over again. After the first big headlines, nothing else had been reported about the murder in the newspaper. She wished so much that the case would be solved! Especially at night, she was afraid that something might happen again. In the past, she'd often left all the windows wide open, always feeling completely safe at home. Now, however, every small crackling sound in the garden or on the roof frightened her. When her daughter Barbara was out and about, she was constantly worried. What's more, a terrible thought kept haunting her. Could Kevin, the father of her own children, have something to do with the murder? Why did he react so strangely, and almost choked, when she told him about that wristwatch? She had loved him and still considered him a very dear friend even after their divorce. These secret thoughts and doubts were driving her crazy! But she didn't dare to speak openly about those suspicions to anyone, especially not to Kevin. After all, they had always trusted each other! It would destroy their relationship – once and for all – if she were to approach him with such an accusation.

Kevin had no idea what Julie was going through. But he too was distressed as the body had been found so close to her home. Did she and their children have a ruthless killer in their neighborhood? Would the police ever find the culprit? Nobody had even come up with a motive for the crime yet. Everyone who knew Lesley seemed to have liked her.

Anna was already mulling over a new idea. If the builder was innocent, then who else could have poisoned Lesley? Did the death of her husband have anything to do with the murder case? Maybe it hadn't been an accident back then? Perhaps Lesley had found out something and had confronted someone, too angry to sense how dangerous that was? Did the police investigate Lesley's past at all?

Anna decided to talk it over with her brother. Although he was still quite young and sometimes acted like a silly child, he also had some good ideas. Sitting in his room, they debated the issue at length.

Finally, Anna said: 'I want to become a detective!'

Sebastian laughed aloud.

'The other day you wanted to become a park ranger!' He reminded her.

Barbara came over for a visit the next evening. She sat down on the porch with Anna, both enjoying the sunset. The entire landscape was bathed in a golden light, the crickets chirped, and the atmosphere was peaceful.

'Do you ever feel depressed?' Anna asked her friend. 'Every once in a while, I feel so sad – everything seems pointless, and yet I should really be satisfied with my life.'

Barbara looked at her thoughtfully.

'I was often sad and upset when my parents had arguments, and completely shocked when they actually divorced. But really depressed? I don't think so.'

'Well, these bad moods only happen occasionally, and once I pull myself together and do something, they usually disappear. For example, it helps if I go for a bicycle tour or for a nice walk.'

Seeing Barbara's concerned expression, Anna smiled.

'Don't worry, I'm not suicidal! I am much too curious to find out what the future has in store for me.'

Barbara responded, 'That's a relief! But please call me at any time if you are feeling sad and need some help!'

The girls spontaneously hugged each other. They had become even closer since their grisly discovery, and Anna was glad that she could talk to her about everything with such ease. Her little brother would probably not really understand her dark moods. She wondered whether Scott would be able to empathize with her.

'Do you think Lesley could have killed herself? After all, she's supposed to have been very depressed since the death of her husband,' Barbara mused. 'Perhaps she also suffered from insomnia because of her depression. Maybe she took sleeping pills on a regular basis. Who knows, she might have experimented with other drugs as well.'

'Nah, I can't imagine it was suicide! Impossible! If it were, then why would somebody else cover her with mud? And why was her body at Stumers Creek in Coolum Beach? She lived in Peregian Beach.'

'Yeah, you are right! Umm, none of it makes any sense,' Barbara said.

Then she continued in a more cheerful tone:

'By the way, I read about an art class in Peregian Beach, starting next week, on Thursday. It will be in the evening, from 6 to 8 pm. Should we sign up for it?'

Anna liked the idea, and they were lucky to get the last available places.

Barbara's mother drove the girls to their first art class and told them that she would also pick them up. She was surprised that the course took place in a private house that had been partly transformed into a small school. The art teacher was named Jeremy and looked like a hippie. He had very long black, somewhat shaggy hair, wore a colorful T-shirt with parrots on it, slightly baggy shorts and old sandals. His skin was darkly tanned and he had almost black eyes, which usually twinkled merrily. Besides Anna and Barbara there were a few other teenage girls in the class, several ladies of varying ages, one boy about 17 years old, and two elderly men.

Barbara was infatuated with Jeremy. He had a nice disposition and devoted a lot of time to each student, and he praised her exuberantly for her first drawing, a sketch with a pencil. She had always enjoyed arts, but had no knowledge of any specific drawing techniques. Now she was eager to learn them. Anna enjoyed drawing too, but she preferred to paint with watercolors and was looking forward to the next classes.

Unfortunately, the next week Barbara was sick with the flu and could not attend the class. Anna was happy when her dad offered to drive her that evening so that she didn't have to cycle alone in the darkness. In the school building she sat down next to Sarah, a middle-aged, chubby woman with a friendly smile, red curls and radiant blue eyes. Sarah had drawn a face with charcoal and red chalk pencil at home, which she now showed to the teacher to ask for his opinion on it.

Anna looked at it and was instantly shocked. She exclaimed:

'This looks so much like a drawing by Lesley! You know, the woman who got killed!' Then she turned bright red, upset about her spontaneous outburst.

Sarah was surprised. 'Oh, did you know Lesley? I'd met her in another class in Noosa once, learning how to draw portraits. How do you know about her artwork?'

Anna swallowed, not sure what to say. Finally, she confessed that she'd recently gone with others to the partially destroyed house where they had found two pictures. Jeremy looked at her oddly for a moment before studying Sarah's drawing.

'Very good!' he praised. 'However, a little bit of the forehead is missing here, and as a result the head is too small.'

With a few quick pencil strokes, he drew the proportions of a face on a piece of paper to illustrate what he meant. Anna watched him in bewilderment. Why had Jeremy looked so grim for a second? Surely, he couldn't care less that they had entered Lesley's house, even if they had acted illegally. Or was he afraid that they might have discovered something there?

Later on, she chatted a bit with Sarah while they drew a bouquet of flowers in a vase.

Sarah told her: 'It seems Lesley was quite introverted. She was a nice lady, always very friendly and respectful to the customers in the store. Apparently, she led a rather secluded life, spending a lot of time gardening, drawing, and making pottery.'

'Did she also have a Datura plant in the garden?' Anna asked.

'Oh, I don't know! She did show me a pencil drawing of a pretty Angel's trumpet, though,' Sarah replied thoughtfully. 'Yeah, I read about that toxic tea and the sleeping pills. Dreadful, isn't it?'

'I wonder why Lesley was killed!' Anna said.

Jeremy apparently overheard her remark, and once again, his dark eyes seemed to flash angrily.

Chapter 9

Sebastian had come home from the rugby game exhausted, bleeding on his elbow and completely filthy. Once again, he was upset about James from the opposing team who had kicked his knee with full intention, unfortunately unnoticed by the referee!

'I wish I were bigger and stronger! Like Peter! Perhaps then James and his friends wouldn't always gang up on me! James is such a nasty guy!' he complained.

Anna giggled. 'Remember the weird name of Peter's rugby team? The wild pigs?'

Trying to take Sebastian's mind off his frustration, Anna told him that Aunt Paula, Uncle Sam and their dogs Lola and Missy would come for a visit that weekend.

'Great!' Sebastian beamed, immediately forgetting his anger towards James and the referee. Just like Anna, he was very fond of these relatives and their two dogs.

On Saturday afternoon, they could hear the booming laughter of their uncle as soon as he and Paula arrived in their old, rusty car. At first, Susi was quite nervous to meet their dogs Lola and Missy, both of them a bit bigger than herself. Missy was a long-legged mongrel with a silky brown fur, a beautifully shaped head and lovely eyes; Lola was a dark-haired medium-sized dog, a mix of an Australian kelpie with who knows what else, with huge ears and a playful demeanor. Susi kept her distance, though, and she was also not so sure about that sturdy, loud man who'd just come in. Sam had a huge nose, a bit of a beer belly, strong, large hands and a thick beard. His brown eyes were twinkling in a nice way. Susi cocked her ears when he turned to her, changing his deep voice to a funny high-pitched tone. Seeing Sebastian's bewildered expression, Aunt Paula laughed and explained that this was Sam's typical 'dog voice'. Dogs were very sensitive to people's tones, and such a cheerful sounding 'sing-song' or 'baby-talk' would probably indicate a non-threatening, peaceful person to them. Susi was still hiding behind Sebastian's legs for now. However, she liked Aunt Paula, the biggish lady with the brown curly hair whose voice sounded a little bit like Lizzie's. She had a friendly smile, too.

After some snacks and tea for the humans and fresh water for the dogs, the family went to the beach. As soon as they got there, Susi lost her anxiety, and all three dogs splashed around enthusiastically in the sea. Missy was the bravest of all, plunging into the waves without a second thought. The sky was a wonderful deep blue, and not a single cloud was in sight. Once again, Lizzie was awestruck by the beautiful scenery and the nearly empty beach. She was happy to live here!

It was fairly early in the afternoon, perhaps a bit too sunny for most people. Together with their relatives, the Kuhlmanns took a long walk nevertheless. Uncle Sam was a very humorous guy, making them laugh a lot. He was an excellent speaker, and even Sebastian listened spellbound, captivated by his intriguing stories. Some of them were bizarre! Was it true that you could identify kangaroos by the unique shape of their ears?

Out of a sudden, Anna stopped dead in her tracks, hardly believing her eyes. Horrified, she pointed to their dogs. They had joyfully run ahead and were now curiously circling around something in the sand. Missy barked excitedly.

'There... there's another corpse!' Anna stammered, paralyzed with fear.

The blood seemed to rush loudly in her ears, and her heart was pounding. Her relatives also stopped where they were, and Aunt Paula stifled a scream. Andy felt as if an ice-cold hand was squeezing his heart. There was a man's head indeed, in the shade of a huge beach umbrella! Another dead person?

The next moment, they spotted a little boy who'd been hiding behind a sand hill. Uncle Sam started to laugh, comprehending the situation quicker than the others. The kid had buried his father almost completely in the sand, just for fun. Only the man's head was sticking out! The dogs didn't quite know what to make of it. They ran in ever smaller circles around the head until the man finally stood up. He shook the sand off his body and smiled.

'I was afraid the dogs would lick my face!'

He patted Lola, while Missy and Susi kept looking at him suspiciously, not daring to get too close.

Only later in the evening did Anna and her mother notice that both of them had gotten a slight sunburn. They apparently had more sensitive skin than the others. After dinner, the adults opened a 4-liter container of red wine, called 'Cask Wine'. They all enjoyed the wine, having a fabulous time and sharing many stories. Unfortunately, the next morning they woke up with a bad headache. Aunt Paula fared the worst! Her head was pounding and she could not eat breakfast. She was thankful when Anna and Sebastian offered to take all three dogs for a walk, and she went back to bed for a while.

'Are you feeling sick too?' Sebastian asked his sister on their hike to the beach. 'You're looking a little pale around your nose! Ha ha,' he laughed, 'even though your nose looks pretty burned!'

'Nah, I'm not sick, but I didn't sleep well. That head sticking out of the sand yesterday gave me such a fright! I really thought another dead person was lying there.'

Anna's blue eyes had a fearful expression. And yet, Sebastian also detected a steely determination in them that made him almost shiver.

'I just have to find out what happened. Otherwise, it will haunt me forever!' Anna gazed at her brother.

'Don't take it to your heart!' Sebastian tried to comfort her. 'After all, murders happen every day; even if not right here at our doorstep.'

'Yeah, I know. But I just can't shake off this nagging feeling as if we've missed something. I keep thinking that we are somehow involved in this whole story. Or that we even know the killer! I can't explain it, but it's such an intense feeling! Horrible!'

It suddenly seemed to Sebastian that the sky was getting darker and the air cooler. But when he looked around, there wasn't a cloud to be seen in the clear blue sky.

'Anna, you have a knack for infecting me with your dark thoughts! I felt really creeped out just now!'

He gave his sister a little nudge and pinched her nose.

'Ow!' Anna screamed.

'Oh, sorry, I forgot about your sunburn!' Sebastian said remorsefully.

Anna playfully gave him a slap on the back of the head, and then they ran with the dogs to the water, having fun at the beach and forgetting all their worries for a while.

Chapter 10

The next day, Lizzie attended one of the guided walks of the Sunshine Coast Wildflower Festival. It was an annual event in spring, where experts took small groups of interested people for walks, teaching them about the native flora in a variety of locations. By the time Lizzie reached the meeting point, many people were already gathered on the car park near a forest. Everyone wore sun hats or caps and sunglasses; some wore rugged work booths. Lizzie had to smile about the knee-length socks of some men in shorts. As soon as all registered people had arrived and ticked their names off a list, the three voluntary group leaders introduced themselves, and one of them gave a short explanation about the Wallum heathland. Then they split up in two groups and started their walk.

Even though it was early in the morning, the sun was already beating down on them relentlessly. Lizzie wondered if she would ever get used to the hot weather in Australia. They all walked in single file along a narrow path. They admired the gnarled banksias that had huge, partially brown, partially iridescent green inflorescences. Acacias, melaleucas and eucalyptus trees alternated with flowering shrubs and tall grass-like plants swaying in the wind.

Lizzie had heard that these public guided walks were very popular, and she quickly understood why. It was lovely to be outdoors and to share the love of nature with others. Some wildflowers were stunning, showing a display of bright colours, making an impressive statement even from a distance. Contrarily, the beauty of some tiny, inconspicuous flowers was only noticeable on closer inspection.

'Look, how pretty!' An elderly woman in front of Lizzie bent down and gently bent some sedges to the side to draw attention to a small blue flower.

'Oh, look over here!' another lady shouted, discovering an orchid.

An old man, who reminded Lizzie of a stork because of his very long and thin legs, spent a lot of time taking photos. Again and again, everyone had to wait for him to join the group.

A young man in a blue shirt pulled a face behind his back. 'Oh boy, I'm getting tired of having to wait for him,' he said to Lizzie.

Nevertheless, he smiled. The day was much too beautiful to waste his time being angry.

'That's Harry. He often takes stunning photographs. And he also creates wonderful drawings,' the elderly woman replied.

'Harry is very smart! He knows almost every native plant in the entire area,' their group leader said with admiration. 'He used to work in a plant nursery. Since he's retired, he draws or paints many flowers, trees and insects. And then he sells some of his pictures as postcards.'

Lizzie chuckled. 'Did you recently watch the toad race in Coolum Beach? My kids told me that one of the cane toads was named 'Smart Harry'. However, he wasn't the fastest toad around, either.'

They all laughed, and even the man in the blue shirt was more willing to wait for the 'Slow Harry'.

Lizzie couldn't remember any botanical names, but she learned a bit about the native plants anyway. She thoroughly enjoyed the walk. Furthermore, she also got to see a Tawny Frogmouth. It actually was a bird! Just like Anna, she had been amused by the name 'Frogmouth Street' when she'd first heard it. Harry spotted the bird on a branch of a Paperbark tree, despite its amazing camouflage.

A few days later, Lizzie attended another organized Sunshine Coast Wildflower Walk. This time, she went to a rainforest near Cooroy. There were several volunteers and twenty-nine participants. Everybody was fascinated by the big trees, rising high into the sky, and their huge buttress roots, extending from the forest floor. Since it had rained the night before, the air was still heavy from the moisture. Thick droplets glistened on the leaves. Lizzie loved the rich green hues of the ferns, the palm trees, and the many different rainforest plants in this shady forest. The impenetrable tangle of lushly growing climbing plants made it look like a jungle to her. Some native Wisterias had twining vines as thick as tree trunks.

Once again, 'Slow Harry' was part of the group and took heaps of photos. In one location along the track, he was studying the fresh shoots of a plant sprouting from an old, fallen tree trunk.

'How beautiful!' Lizzie exclaimed. 'New life out of dead wood! And look at the lovely pattern on the bark!'

Harry asked her, 'Are you also interested in drawing?'

'No, but my daughter is! Anna is actually enrolled in an art class in Peregian Beach,' Lizzie replied. 'The teacher is supposed to be very good.'

'That has to be Jeremy! I know him. He prefers to paint abstract things in bright oil colors, which I personally find hideous. But he can also draw wonderful, realistic pictures. I've been to one of his exhibitions and was surprised at how diverse his works were.'

He painstakingly cleaned his glasses and continued:

'By the way, did you know that he was good friends with Lesley? You must have heard of the woman who was murdered in Coolum Beach, right?'

'Yes, I did! And can you imagine? My own daughter and her friend Barbara discovered her body on a walk! It was such as shock! The girls still haven't gotten over it. Just recently Anna thought she saw the head of a dead person on the beach! Luckily, she was mistaken! But I feel so sorry for her as she constantly has nightmares. I wish they'd finally catch the killer! Maybe then Anna will be able to get a good night's sleep again.'

'Yeah, I hope so, too. What a dreadful story!' Harry looked sad.

'Oh dear, we have to hurry up, the others are already waiting for us.'

The two quickly set off again. Only later did they realize that they were not the last ones to catch up with the group. Back at the original meeting point, one of the group leaders checked off the names on the list of participants. And he noticed that one woman was missing!

They all started talking frantically at the same time.

'Who's missing? What did she look like? We have to go back and find her!'

Lizzie was in utter shock. What had happened? Another murder? She shuddered. And then she realized that she was acting like Anna, instantly fearing the worst. The guides were horrified and blamed themselves. How could anybody get lost during the hike? Usually, one of them stayed at the rear of the group to prevent this from happening. However, they tried to be calm and in control. One man advised the other participants to go home. Reluctantly, four women and three men left, because they had to return to work. But everyone else stayed, wanting to help find the missing person.

'Okay, let's form three groups,' one of the biologists decided resolutely. 'One group will go back the same way we came, and the other groups will check the other main trails. It would be best if you, Mary and Jim, could wait here in the parking lot. Just in case the woman should find the way here by herself! Her name is Marie, by the way.'

Mary and Jim nodded. They were members of a regional environmental organization.

Mary suggested: 'Whoever happens to find Marie should immediately call someone in the other groups. Who's got a mobile phone?'

Just then a man shouted, 'There she is! Yay!'

The missing woman came from a completely different direction than Lizzie would have expected.

'Hi Marie! We all got so worried about you!' said Jim.

'I got lost!' Marie replied and smiled sheepishly. 'Right at the beginning, I discovered an interesting giant mushroom glowing on a tree trunk. I went over to have a closer look at it. And then I somehow ended up on the wrong trail! Um, I didn't know where I was anymore. The path became very narrow and even came to an end, and I had to bush-bash for a while. I actually got a bit scared among the huge ferns and shrubs. But thank God I came across one of the main trails again.'

She brushed her hair off her forehead.

'And here I am! Gosh, I'm glad I found my way back!'

'So am I!' said the biologist and grinned.

Lizzie clapped her hands, and then the whole crowd whistled and applauded. Marie's face turned bright red.

Chapter 11

Anna and Barbara were on the way to the next painting class, cycling beside each other on a pedestrian path than ran parallel to the street. They had passed the residential areas near Mount Emu and were now surrounded by forest. Due to a recent small bushfire the air was still smelling smoky.

'Do you think Jeremy could have something to do with Lesley's murder? My mother told me that he was friends with her,' Anna called out to Barbara.

Barbara shouted back, 'No way! Are you crazy? He's super nice!'

'Well, he scowled when he heard we were at Lesley's house the other day. For a moment he looked like he wanted to kill me!'

'I would be angry too if someone snooped around in our house,' Barbara defended their teacher.

She was well again but still looking a bit pale, and she cycled more slowly than she usually did. When they finally reached the classroom, almost every seat was already taken. Anna looked around and shared a table with an older woman, and Barbara sat down next to a handsome boy. She grinned cheekily at Anna as if to say that she had got the better spot. Today they painted with watercolors for the first time. They learned how to moisten the special watercolor paper and did some experiments, mixing different colours and trying out special effects. Anna became completely immersed in her work, painting enthusiastically in flowing movements.

When Jeremy came over to her, he said, 'Well done! Anna, you seem to have a talent for this, and a good eye for colour! I really like the flow of wavy lines. You are very creative!'

Anna smiled gratefully and proudly. Glancing at Barbara, she noticed that her friend was talking to the boy at her table animatedly, and that her cheeks had got some color again.

Later, on their way back home, Barbara said enthusiastically, 'I am glad I got to sit beside Phil, he is such a nice guy!'

'What were you talking about?' Anna asked curiously. 'You two were talking up a storm!'

'All sorts of things,' Barbara replied. 'Phil wants to study graphic design. He is taking this art class to prepare himself for his portfolio. But I think he already is quite a skilled artist! And he has really beautiful hands – very strong and yet so slender and delicate ...'

Anna grinned broadly. 'So, you've fallen head over heels for him, huh? I thought you had fallen in love with Jeremy!'

Barbara hemmed and hawed for a while, fiddling around with the straps of her bicycle helmet. Finally, she admitted that she thought Phil was fantastic.

Then she added, 'You know what? His mother is also in our painting class. She is the pretty woman with the long blond hair who was wearing the bright red dress today. Her name is Jane. The funny thing is, they both have very similar styles when it comes to painting! And as a kind of a trial, they have decided to sit apart from each other so that nobody could say they would copy from each other. But still, each time their pictures look very similar. Weird, hey? Phil is quite intrigued by that himself, and he seems to be very fond of his mother.'

'Interesting! I'll have to look at their paintings next time!' Anna said.

She pedalled a bit faster, breathing in the fresh sea air that mingled with a faint smell of burnt wood and other scents of the forest. The waves were roaring loudly behind the dunes. And suddenly she was filled with the desire to see Scott again. She longed to chat and laugh with him, to hug him and to touch his smooth skin. How would it be to kiss him, and to be caressed by him?

As if Barbara could read her mind, she asked,

'When will you see Scott again?'

Anna sighed. 'I don't know yet. But Sebastian and I are definitely going to spend our Christmas holidays with Aunt

Paula and Uncle Sam again, and that's close to Scott's home. I can't wait to see him, and the others as well, you know, Susan, Mike and Kylie. It's a shame that you can't come with us, too.'

Sebastian was also looking forward to the summer vacation. But he was too busy to think much about it. Time flew by with soccer and rugby games, dog walks, cycling and swimming. He even enjoyed school most of the time, although homework was often annoying. One thing was sure, though, he didn't like one of his teachers at all. She was very pretty, but a 'wicked witch', as he privately described her. Besides being very strict, she could give the students such a scornful look that they felt very humiliated and inferior. Unfortunately, she was his teacher for two subjects, namely English and History. Since Sebastian had a rather strong German accent, she had made fun of him on several occasions, sometimes even making nasty comments. Although Sebastian was normally a happy and outgoing boy, he hardly dared to say a word in front of her. He hated Mrs. Jane!

Strangely enough, she had offered the students to address her by her first name, after her title. Calling others by their first names was common practice in Australia, but usually that didn't apply to teachers. However, Anna also called her art teacher 'Jeremy'. Maybe Mrs. Jane wasn't too fond of her somewhat odd last name? It was 'Punch', a word which could define both a drink and a blow with the fist. The majority of his classmates feared this teacher as much as Sebastian did. All of them were afraid to make a tiny sound, breathing a sigh of relief as soon as the class was over.

Sebastian's favorite teacher was Mr. Smithfield who taught Chemistry. He was quite the opposite of Mrs. Jane. When someone made a mistake, he calmly and objectively explained what was wrong, and he always praised the students whenever they did something right. Although there was a lot to learn and it could be difficult to understand the mathematical formulas, Sebastian enjoyed this subject, especially the hands-on lab experiments. This teacher made the chemistry lessons very interesting. Somehow, he had a knack for motivating his students instead of just giving long boring lectures.

His gym teacher, Mr. Harris, was okay too. He looked quite old but was physically fit, well-toned, and extremely funny. He was really nice, even encouraging those pupils who were not very sporty. Unlike Sebastian's former gym teacher in Germany, who only ever wanted to train the most athletic students.

One sunny day in September, Sebastian's class went on a school trip to the Tanawha Botanical Garden by bus. Their biology teacher was in charge, and Mrs. Jane and an art teacher also attended the excursion. Sebastian had expected a park with man-made flower beds and was surprised to see a natural-looking forest with a lake.

'Hey, look at that!' Jack shouted in amazement as they entered the bushland.

'Shh!' hissed Mrs. Jane. 'Be quiet, don't scare it away!'

Directly in front of them stood a deer! It didn't seem to be bothered by them at all, but was curiously looking at them from its velvety brown eyes. The students walked quietly past the stately animal and deeper into the forest. After a while Mr. Longboat, their biology teacher, asked them to stop and gather around him, and he explained that feral deer were regarded as a significant pest in Australia. They had been introduced from Europe and Asia by European settlers in the 19th century as game animals. Now they were causing increasing damages both to the native environment and to agricultural businesses. They would compete with kangaroos, wallabies and grazing farm animals, eat saplings, herbs, bark and leaves, and occasionally also fruit. They would often trample plants, rub themselves against trees, and thus damaging them, and they could also contribute to erosion and spread weed seeds.

'But they're so cute!' the art teacher whispered to Mrs. Jane.

Sebastian loved this forest. Everything was beautifully green and, in a way, looking enchanted. Mr. Longboat was busy pointing out certain animals and plants along the way. Sebastian was impressed with the giant ferns on enormous tree stumps, and the palms illuminated by the light, while his friend Jack showed more interest in the animals. Jack discovered all sorts of unusual beetles. He was delighted with a green moth, perched on a leaf of exactly the same color. A few times they heard rustling in the bushes. Was it a snake, a lizard, or some other animal? Sebastian steered as far away from Mrs. Jane as possible, and yet he heard her joking and laughing out loud with Miss Perrington, the art teacher. Was it possible the 'wicked witch' could be nice?

Eventually the group came to an area where sculptures by various artists were on display. Sebastian and Jack thought a snake on a rock was especially pretty. It was only when they took a second look that they discovered a small frog on it – food for the snake. From a distance you could almost believe that the animals were real. Miss Perrington assembled all of the students around her and talked about the impressive sculptures, while Mr. Longboat was already looking for more animals in the bushes.

On the way home on the bus, Jack and Sebastian sat right behind Mrs. Jane and Miss Perrington. After walking around for several hours, the boys were quite tired and dozed off. But all of a sudden, Sebastian was wide awake again, listening eagerly to the female teachers.

Chapter 12

'Hey, Anna, I overheard something really interesting from my nasty teacher on the bus today,' Sebastian said cheerfully, while he was searching for a snack in the kitchen.

'What did you hear? And which teacher?' Anna frowned. Sometimes she had difficulties following her brother's quick flow of words.

'Mrs. Jane! She was talking to our art teacher and mentioned Jeremy, the teacher in your painting class.'

'Yeah, and ...? So what?' Anna asked, now a little more curious.

'Jeremy was in love with Lesley! She said he was devastated when he found out about her murder. But now he is in a relationship with Mrs. Jane. With that bitch!'

'Now, now, Sebastian, watch what you say!' his mother interjected, who was just coming into the kitchen.

'Sorry!' Sebastian muttered.

'What does Mrs. Jane look like?' Anna wanted to know.

'She is quite tall and beautiful, with long blond hair. Pretty slender but very muscular. She looks like she goes to the gym and works out every day. And she always wears bright clothes …' Sebastian took a bite of a chocolate muesli bar, 'and often her hat and her shoes have the same colour.'

Sebastian babbled away, sharing everything that popped into his mind. Anna suddenly connected the dots.

'That could be Phil's mother,' she blurted out. 'They are both in Jeremy's art class. Um, are her fingernails painted black?'

Sebastian was perplexed. 'Yes, they are, at least at the moment! Earlier, they were bright red, I think, and before that dark purple. So, you know her too! Wow, that's something else! Have you ever spoken to this woman?'

'No, but Barbara recently sat next to her son and thinks he's fabulous,' Anna replied and grinned.

'Oh boy, with a mother like that?' Sebastian asked doubtfully and made a face.

'No Susi, you can't have chocolates! They would make you sick!' he said to the dog who was begging him for food, giving it a pat.

'Susi has the most beautiful eyes!' Anna said lovingly and petted her too.

'Better don't encourage her to beg, though!' Lizzie advised.

She smiled, inwardly admitting that it was not always easy to be a firm and consistent dog trainer. They were all totally smitten with their Susi!

*　*　*

A few days later, Susi was overjoyed to get a new four-legged friend. Lizzie and Andy had become members of the 'Moist Nose Rescue'. They would temporarily foster other dogs – just one at a time as they already took care of Susi. This organization helped to re-home many cats and dogs whose owners could no longer look after them, for whatever reason. It could be a serious health problem or death, or financial issues. In many cases, the organization also rescued animals that had been abused or simply abandoned.

Now Lizzie had picked up her first foster dog, a pug named Frank. His owner had moved to a nursing home and was unable to take him there. Lizzie liked Frank instantly, he was so cute! When Andy saw him, he had to laugh involuntarily. What a funny looking puppy! Frank was only about one year old and very playful. It did not take long for him and Susi to romp around and race through the house and garden. They had a wonderful time together! However, Frank was not yet completely house-trained, so Lizzie kept both dogs in the back garden for most of the day.

The first night that Frank stayed with them, Anna woke up from an eerie crying sound. It was the pug! He apparently felt lonely, despite lying on a comfortable cushion, right next to Susi in the living room. Poor Frankie! Anna thought. He must be missing his beloved owner and familiar surroundings! She petted him for a while, and finally he calmed down and eventually fell into a deep sleep. Later that night she heard him crying again, but she didn't want him to think that she would come running to him every time he did that. And luckily, he soon stopped. But a few minutes later, he started snoring loudly, waking up the whole family. Incredible that a small dog could make such a noise! He also emitted funny grunting sounds during the day, making them all laugh out loud.

Frank was a very nice and friendly dog, and within the next week many people inquired about him, willing to adopt him. The manager of the 'Moist Nose Rescue' organization decided to give Frank to a family who already had another young pug and a cat and who seemed to take good care of their pets. Of course, the Kuhlmanns were very sad to let little Frank go! On the other hand, they were happy about the successful re-homing. Lizzie was delighted when Frank's new owners sent her photos of the two pugs and the cat the next day, all cuddling together. It seemed Frank had found a great new family! And the Kuhlmanns were looking forward to getting their new foster dog.

*　*　*

During their next art class, Barbara once again took a seat next to Phil. Anna had asked her to find out a bit more about his mother, as discreetly as possible. Barbara was curious herself and didn't mind chatting to him anyway. Anna dared to sit down beside Mrs. Jane, even though Sebastian had told her so many terrible things about this woman. Anna kept peeking at her, hoping that she wouldn't notice. Mrs. Jane was very beautiful indeed, with a delicately shaped face, silky shiny hair and long, elegant legs. She had a slim, yet quite muscular body and surprisingly broad shoulders. Was she possibly a swimmer? Anna was a little surprised that she had never noticed this teacher in school before.

'That's a very pretty landscape!' Anna said to her, looking at her postcard. Today, everyone had brought a card to copy from. 'Where is this?'

'It's a river scene in North Queensland,' Mrs. Jane replied in a friendly and pleasant voice. 'Beautiful, isn't it? But I am glad that there are no crocodiles here on the Sunshine Coast!' She chuckled softly. 'You have an interesting accent. Do you come from Germany?'

'Yes, my little brother Sebastian is a student of yours,' Anna blurted out, at the same moment feeling angry with herself. How stupid of her to admit that she already knew something about her! Wishing to be able to take back her words, she fiddled around with her paint brushes.

Mrs. Jane responded kindly, 'Oh yes, Sebastian. He struggles a bit with English grammar and pronunciation, but he does very well in History!'

Anna actually thought Mrs. Jane was quite nice. And yet, Sebastian constantly complained about her! Well, some people seemed to be completely different persons in their private life than at their workplace. However, Mrs. Jane did exude a certain coldness and arrogance, and her blue eyes reminded Anna of a lifeless doll.

Soon she forgot about the world around her as she started her painting in A3 size, using the landscape on her postcard as a guide. It had been a card from a German friend, depicting a rushing river in Bavaria. She loved painting with watercolors! But it was tricky to improve something because the colours always shone through and you couldn't just paint over a mistake. She wasn't quite happy with the rocks.

Jeremy came to their table and studied Anna's art work.

'That's fantastic, Anna!' he praised her. 'Your colours and the bubbling water are wonderful! Only the rocks look a bit fake. Better don't use black in the future, it makes things too dark!'

Then he inspected Mrs. Jane's work. 'These crocodiles look even more dangerous in your big picture than on the little postcard!'

He smiled, took the brush from her hand and showed her on his own watercolour pad how she could improve the shadow of a tree to make it appear more realistic. He touched her hand lightly and looked at her lovingly for a moment.

Meanwhile, Barbara was a bit disappointed as Phil didn't reveal much about his mother. All she learned was that his parents had already separated when he was only 10 years old. Since then, he had seldom seen his father, and his mother spoke of him with great hatred. Phil was quite impressed that Barbara's parents still got on so well despite their divorce.

However, recently Barbara had sensed something odd about her parents, but she would rather discuss this with Anna than with Phil. Cycling home, she said to Anna: 'You know what's strange? Lately, my mom seems to be kind of tense when my dad comes to visit us. I wonder why?'

'Maybe she has a boyfriend and doesn't want to admit it yet?' Anna suggested.

Barbara giggled. How would she and her siblings get along with such a man? The idea that a stranger could invade their shared life was weird.

When Anna told her brother later that evening that she had chatted quite amiably with Mrs. Jane and did not find her terrible, Sebastian was utterly astonished. Apparently, Mrs. Jane could be a nicer person if she only wanted to. Nevertheless, Anna admitted that she had felt a little uncomfortable around her.

Chapter 13

The sun was beating down on them while Barbara and her father were playing tennis. They had rented a tennis court at the Coolum Sports Complex for one hour.

'You are mean!' Barbara cried out indignantly.

Her father had just sent her from corner to corner and won the match. Both were bright red in the face, sweaty and exhausted, but feeling great. It had been fun, although they were not the best players by any means. To cool off a bit, they drove to a nearby lookout point by the sea and drank a fruit juice there. A fresh breeze blew in their faces. Barbara enjoyed having her father all to herself for once.

'Have you ever had a girlfriend since Mum broke up with you?' she asked him, thinking that he was still quite an attractive man. He was tall and muscular with an open, friendly face and warm brown eyes. She didn't even mind his hooked nose at all, while she detested the shape of her own nose that was so similar to his.

Kevin looked a little embarrassed. 'Um, well, I did have a brief relationship once,' he said, fidgeting around with his drinking bottle.

'Oh, really, with whom?' asked Barbara, her interest piqued.

'There was this teacher in your school. I'm not sure if you know Jane, um, Mrs. Punch.'

Barbara was astonished.

'You mean Mrs. Jane? Anna and I were talking about her only recently! And she is with us in Jeremy's art class!'

She considered telling him about Phil, Mrs. Jane's son, for a moment, but instead she just asked, 'How did you two meet? And what went wrong?'

'I met her in a pub one day and fell head over heels in love with her. She is so beautiful! But after a while I noticed that she is really bitchy and domineering. We started arguing a lot and it was much worse than it was with your mother.' Kevin sighed. 'It seems that I have no luck with women!'

'Unlucky in love but lucky at games!' Barbara laughed. 'You have won the tennis match against me today and you won some money on that cane toad race the other day.'

Kevin chuckled. 'Yeah, that was nice! Although Julie hates gambling. She always told me how silly it would be to lose money on a bet. But I never put up much money anyway, it's just a bit of fun with my friends, and I'd never gamble in a Casino or something like that. Come on, let's go home and take a shower! Otherwise, we'll catch a cold from being out in this wind.'

He brought his daughter to Julie's place and then drove on to his own little home. Under the soothing hot shower, Kevin wondered if he could have lost his old watch at Jane's house when he had left her in a hurry. Back then, they had spent a romantic evening and a passionate, erotic night together. But the next morning, they had suddenly got into a nasty verbal fight that was much worse than any former arguments between them. In the end, he had stormed out of her house in a fury. He could hardly believe how malicious and insulting she'd become, treating him like trash. Her facial features had been so distorted that he'd almost been afraid of her, even though she had seemed to have been so full of love and devotion the night before.

Only later did he notice that his watch was gone. But he was not quite sure whether he had really lost it at Jane's place or somewhere else, because the leather watch band was quite old and brittle and it could have happened anywhere. Nevertheless, when he heard from Julie that Anna's dog Susi had found a watch at the creek, very close to the crime scene, he was shocked. Could it be his watch? After all, Barbara had indicated that the watch band looked similar. But how could it have landed there? Should he ask Jane if she had found his watch in her bedroom? Oh no, he didn't want to see her again – and neither her son, because Phil had come across as extremely arrogant.

Barbara found it hard to fathom that her dad had been in a relationship with Mrs. Jane. Somehow feeling uneasy about it, she went into her room and decided to call Anna. After sharing her new information, Barbara begged her:

'Please don't tell my mother or my siblings any of this!'

Barbara wondered how her mother would react if she were to learn of her ex-husband's love affair. Or maybe she already knew what was going on, without telling her children? Barbara wished she'd asked her father how long he had actually been together with Mrs. Jane.

Anna kept her promise not to break the news to Barbara's family, but she told her brother about Kevin's relationship with Mrs. Jane.

'No way!' Sebastian was dumbfounded. 'Thank goodness he found out how mean she can be! I bet Barbara and her siblings wouldn't have liked to deal with her!'

Considering the beauty of Mrs. Jane, Anna could easily understand why Kevin had fallen in love with her. And now their art teacher was evidently dating Mrs. Jane. How would that work out? Although she barely knew either of them, she felt sorry for Jeremy.

*　*　*

Barbara was sitting with Phil at a sidewalk café, drinking a banana milkshake from a huge glass. She was a bit nervous and self-conscious, especially with regards to her Roman nose. Would Phil find her pretty in spite of her hooked nose? He was in a good mood, making jokes and laughing a lot. But suddenly his expression changed as he noticed Kevin on the pedestrian path, walking at a brisk pace. That guy had once been in a relationship with his mother, and he couldn't stand him! Luckily, he seemed to be in a hurry and might not see him.

'Hi, Dad!' Barbara called out. 'What are you doing here?'

Her father stopped and frowned. Why was his daughter sitting here with Phil? Both men stared at each other with animosity for a moment. Then Kevin pulled himself together and said,

'Phil, how are you doing? I see that you and my daughter are friends.'

'Hello, Kevin! Yes, we met in an art class. Barbara is very talented. I didn't know that she's your daughter.'

Barbara blushed and didn't know what to say. Thankfully, her father explained he had an important appointment to go to, and he left. However, Phil seemed to be gloomy now, and there was an awkward silence. Then they both started talking at the same time, but the cheerful mood from before had vanished. Barbara was mad. Why did her father have to show up just now?

Bad luck! And why would they both look at each other so grimly?

Phil was angry too. He had enjoyed flirting with Barbara, a very attractive girl who obviously adored him. What a bummer that Kevin, of all the people in the world, was her father! However, he had to admit that he'd never liked any of his mother's many lovers. Only her new boyfriend, Jeremy, seemed to be okay, although he sometimes acted a bit freaky. Just to think of Jeremy's ridiculous brightly colored T-shirts, the crappy sandals and his long shaggy hair! His slightly unkempt appearance contrasted with his beautiful, elegant mother whom he'd always adored.

Well, she also loves bright colors, he thought, and they are both interested in art. Would it be more than a brief affair this time? What was most important to him was that Jeremy left him alone and that he didn't have that fatherly attitude towards him! The paternal behaviour of his mother's former boyfriends had infuriated him.

Kevin wasn't happy as he walked away from the café, deep in thought. Did Barbara have an intimate relationship with Phil? She had never mentioned his name! But at that age, girls frequently had a crush on boys and didn't necessarily tell their parents about it. At the same time, he was annoyed that he had not taken advantage of this opportunity to ask Phil about his lost watch. Perhaps he should go to the police and ask if he could see the watch band that his daughter and Anna had found at Stumers Creek? Oh no, better not!

His thoughts were spinning in circles until he abruptly came to a halt. A woman close behind him crashed into him, letting out a small scream.

'Oh, please excuse me!' Kevin mumbled, embarrassed, and hurried on.

A terrible suspicion suddenly filled his mind. Could Phil be the murderer? Had he killed Lesley at the creek and then tried to frame him for the crime, just because he didn't like him? Had Phil purposely destroyed Kevin's old watch so that it would stop at the exact time of death, pointing to Kevin as the culprit? The next moment, Kevin decided that this idea was absurd. What reason could Phil possibly have had to kill Lesley? Besides, Phil definitely knew that he wasn't living with Julie near the crime scene any more. Since he'd moved away more than a year ago, Kevin just visited Julie and the kids from time to time.

A new thought occurred to Kevin, making him feel sick. Perhaps Jane had something to do with the murder? Did she want revenge on him, leaving his watch near the corpse so that he would be a prime suspect? But then he shook his head. Although it had been quite an unusual, handmade Moroccan leather band that he'd bought on the Eumundi Market once, it didn't make sense to use that as an indicator. Furthermore,

Barbara had only pointed out that the watch band at the creek had looked similar to his.

And what could have been Jane's motive for wanting to kill Lesley? Had she even known her? Just by chance, talking to a neighbor the day before, Kevin had found out that Jeremy, Barbara's art teacher, had been Lesley's partner for a while and that he was now seeing an English teacher. Could that be Jane? Had she poisoned Lesley so she could be together with Jeremy? Kevin shuddered and got goosebumps. Just when he started to get a grip on himself after all the difficult times with Julie and their divorce, his head was spinning again. Was he going nuts?

Chapter 14

One morning in October, Anna got up very early. She hadn't slept well and blamed the full moon for her restless night. Sebastian was already up, ready to go for a walk with their dog. Susi jumped up on them enthusiastically and couldn't wait to get going. She was a sheer bundle of energy!

'I might as well start taking Susi for walks at night since I can't sleep anyway,' Anna said to her brother and yawned heartily.

'Oh yeah, that's a great idea! Let's do that!' Sebastian replied.

The next night, the siblings snuck out of the house, careful not to wake up their parents. They would certainly have forbidden them to go out at night. Sebastian was only 12 years old and Anna wasn't yet 15. Fortunately, Susi almost never barked and was also quiet now, and so they managed to leave the house unnoticed by Andy and Lizzie.

The beach was deserted, and the waves roared loudly, their sound intensified at night when everything else was silent. The sea shone silver in the moonlight. However, Susi had no time for romantic thoughts. As soon as she was off the leash, she chased after a crab that was scurrying around. But it disappeared into a hole before she could catch it. Anna and Sebastian walked on the hard sand by the water, avoiding the waves because they had their sneakers on.

'Last night, when I'd trouble sleeping, I had a new idea,' Anna said. 'Lesley could have owned some expensive paintings by famous artists, and also some valuable antiques in her house. Maybe Jeremy wanted to get them? Therefore, he pretended to be her friend, and then he killed her so that he could steal everything at his leisure. He only left behind the works she had painted herself, those small pictures that we have seen in her house.'

'Or perhaps he killed her because she caught him stealing red-handed!' Sebastian said excitedly.

They detected a glow of light in the distance. Someone had made a small fire on the beach. As they approached, they could see that a couple was embracing each other by the fire. It was Jeremy and Mrs. Jane!

'Oh no!' Sebastian moaned. 'Even in the middle of the night I have to run into my horrible teacher, of all people!'

Anna grinned. 'Yeah, it's a small world! The other day Barbara saw her father while she was sitting with Phil in a café. That chance encounter really upset her, because it totally spoiled their mood.'

'Is Phil her boyfriend now?' Sebastian asked curiously.

'Nope! At first, she was all excited about him, and she met up with him a couple more times, but now she says that he is too arrogant and conceited. He is good-looking, but not nearly as nice as she thought.'

'See, I told you so!' Sebastian said triumphantly. 'Somehow I couldn't imagine anybody with a mother like that would be a nice person!'

'Shh, not so loud!' Anna admonished him. 'Otherwise, Mrs. Jane might hear you!'

'Come on, we'd better head back!' Sebastian softly whistled for Susi to come, and she obediently ran up to them, with an old tennis ball in her mouth that she'd found even in the darkness.

October was Andy's favorite month. The temperatures were very pleasant, already quite warm but not yet as humid as they would be from November to February. On one sunny Saturday, the whole family was sitting in the garden, and Barbara was also there. Andy reviewed his electrical installation plans for the proposed apartment building in Peregian Beach. The architect had made some changes to the building design, and therefore Andy had to make some modifications to his plan as well. Bad timing, as he and his partner had already plenty of other work! Sometimes they even had to rush out after business hours. Like last night, when Andy received an emergency call: an electrical hazard in an industrial area required immediate action. Luckily, nobody had been injured, and he could quickly fix the fault. But afterwards he was wide awake, unable to fall asleep. And now he was so tired! He sighed, feeling a bit stressed. But then he thought how lucky he was, being able to do some work from home and having such a great partner. He and Greg got along very well.

Sebastian and Anna went into the kitchen to get some drinks for everybody. Sebastian handed his father a cup of tea and asked him:

'Who is actually the new owner of Lesley's property?'

'I thought it was Ray,' Lizzie said.

'No, Ray is the project manager of the construction company. The owner's name is...' Andy looked at the plan, 'Philip Anderson.'

Barbara exclaimed, 'What? But that's Phil, Mrs. Jane's son!'

'Phil? Are you sure about that?' Anna asked, frowning.

'Yes, he has his father's last name. The name 'Punch' is Jane's maiden name, which she kept after she got married. Phil told me that. And his full first name is Philip.' Barbara was quite agitated.

Everyone was silent.

Then Anna said, 'Hey, maybe I was right about the motive for the murder after all! With the only difference that it wasn't Ray but Phil who was keen on Lesley's property!'

'Is that possible?' Sebastian questioned. 'He's not of legal age yet, is he? I bet his mother is involved!'

Andy and Lizzie looked apprehensive. They didn't like their children talking about the murder all the time, playing detective and making wild accusations. But none of them could forget the gruesome crime, even though it happened a few months ago. And it had to be even worse for Barbara and her family, since the body had been found very close to their home. Andy strictly cautioned the children not to tell anyone about their suspicions.

* * *

The next time Kevin came to pick up Lisa and Tom, Barbara was the only one at home. She told him that her mother and siblings were still out shopping, but would be back soon.

'Dad, can you believe that Phil is the new owner of Lesley's property? Is he already of legal age? I never asked him about his date of birth.'

'What, really? Um, yes, he turned 18 in July. I still remember him throwing a huge birthday party. This is incredible! I didn't even know his parents had so much money! After all, they must have purchased the property for him.'

'Anna and Sebastian believe that Phil and his mother may have killed Lesley in order to buy the profitable acreage,' Barbara blurted out.

Her father turned white as a ghost, shocked about her words. So, he wasn't the only one suspecting Phil and Jane!

At that moment Julie and the children returned from shopping, carrying heavy bags.

'Hi, Kevin! Hello, Dad!' they shouted.

'Kevin, I found your old watch!' Julie beamed at her ex-husband. 'This morning, I finally got around to taking care of the overgrown front garden, and that's where I saw it in the bushes. You must have lost it when you were cutting the one dead branch off the bottlebrush tree!'

Kevin had to sit back down as his legs were feeling like jelly. He had gone crazy over nothing! It wasn't his watch that had been found near the dead body! He shook his head, feeling like an idiot.

His behaviour and his chalky-white face puzzled Julie. And why had he earlier lied to them, saying he had thrown away his old watch? Regardless, she was relieved that the watch found at the crime scene had belonged to someone else! She gave him a big kiss, a smack on the lips, even though they had been divorced for over a year and were actually just good friends now. This made Kevin blush and the children giggle.

Chapter 15

Anna and Sebastian continued to ponder whether Mrs. Jane and her son Phil could really be the culprits. They needed proof! And did the poison of the Datura play a major role? They personally didn't know anybody who experimented with this plant, or with any other drugs. Was it possible that Phil had prepared this deadly 'cocktail' containing the plant poison and sleeping pills for the poor woman? Was he somehow involved in dealing drugs? Or was it his mother, Mrs. Jane Punch, the 'wicked witch'? In some respects, it was a shame that Barbara had broken off all contact with Phil, because otherwise she might have been able to get some useful information out of him. Anna and Barbara could hardly believe that their six-week painting course had passed already. They had enjoyed it immensely and intended to take an advanced course in the near future.

Although Sebastian didn't feel like going, the girls dragged him along to an art exhibition in their local community center one day. A wide variety of paintings, artworks and sculptures by local artists were on display. Barbara was surprised to see that Phil had a small exhibition, too, and she looked at his pictures with interest. Most of them were painted in oils, abstract and very colorful. Jeremy would be thrilled, she thought.

Sebastian inspected some amazing metal work by a pretty young lady, and then he walked to the next table where a skinny senior smiled friendly at him. It was 'Slow Harry', the old man whom Lizzie had met on two guided Sunshine Coast Wildflower Walks. He had created gorgeous postcards and calendars with prints of his own art works, mostly showing landscapes and seascapes, flowers and animals. Sebastian studied his amazing display of crashing waves and sunsets, colorful parrots in trees, butterflies on flowers, and some kite surfers out in the ocean. His mother would probably like the drawing of an elderly lady with a huge hat, sitting on a beautiful wooden bench in a garden. It was a delightful setting, with a natural looking pond and Lotus flowers. A cute looking frog was sitting on one of the huge leaves.

And then Sebastian saw one page of a monthly calendar that almost made him cry out in surprise! It showed two women at a creek who were busy painting. One of them had long blonde hair reaching almost to her hips, the other had almost equally long black hair. Sebastian ran to his sister who was just admiring some extraordinary sculptures. Anna was intrigued by the replicated giant snails whose shells sparkled in dazzling colors. She cast her brother an irritated look as he grabbed her by the arm. He could be so annoying!

'Anna, come quickly! I've discovered something!' Sebastian whispered into her ear and dragged her to the calendar at Harry's table. He watched Anna's face, waiting for her reaction while she was flipping through the pages. When she reached the month in which the two women could be seen by the creek, she gasped.

'That's insane! I can't believe it! Where's Barbara? We have to show her!'

They called Barbara over, and Harry was stunned that the three kids were so interested in his calendar.

'That's the creek close to my home!' Barbara exclaimed. 'I know this weirdly twisted old tree! And that's Mrs. Jane and Lesley painting together! I remember Lesley's face from a picture in the newspaper.'

Suddenly Phil was standing behind her, asking:

'What have you guys found? You look so excited.'

His eyes widened when he recognized his mother in Harry's painting, printed on glossy paper.

'When did you paint this?' he asked the old man.

'Oh, that was a while ago.' Harry scratched his chin thoughtfully. 'Early one morning, at dawn, I went for a long walk, taking many photos of all sorts of things. And then I spotted the two women on the other side of the creek. It looked so picture perfect! And so, I took a photo of them and painted it later on.'

'Did the women see you as well?' Phil inquired.

'No, I don't think so. It appeared to me that they were immersed in their work.'

'But that's Lesley, the poor woman who got killed!' Sebastian blurted out without thinking.

Harry nodded; his expression very sad. 'Yes, what a horrible crime, such a tragedy!'

'Why didn't you show this picture to the police?' Anna asked.

Before Harry could respond, Phil cut in, his tone of voice almost shrill: 'Why should he? My mother went out painting with Lesley one time. So what? They met each other at one of Jeremy's painting classes, and then they hung out from time to time. That's all there is to it.'

Barbara shouted, 'But that's exactly the spot where Lesley was killed!'

The outburst drew the attention of a few other people, all staring at them curiously. Harry's cheeks turned bright red. He never expected his picture to cause such a stir! Phil's face was also red, but out of anger. His eyes narrowed to slits and a deep crease formed above his narrow nose. But before he could say anything, his mother appeared.

'Oh no!' Sebastian thought, startled. Mrs. Jane is here too! Now what? He felt like a rabbit in front of a snake every time he saw her. This reminded him of the small frog sculpture in front of the artificial snake on the rock, the beautiful artwork he'd seen in the Botanical Garden, and he chuckled nervously. Anna looked at him, baffled. Why was he laughing? Just now, at the worst possible moment?

Mrs. Jane took the calendar and studied the picture. Her hands trembled a little, but her voice was calm.

'That's a lovely painting, Harry. I was always under the impression that you only drew insects and plants. Yeah, what happened to Lesley was terrible.' She turned to her son. 'Phil, Laura is interested in one of your pictures. Can you tell her more about it?'

She and Phil walked back to his own display of paintings. The other visitors nearby Harry's table turned their attention to the art show again, obviously not quite understanding the subject matter. Harry and the three teenagers looked at each other awkwardly. What should they do now? After a brief discussion – in hushed whispers – they made a decision. Harry would look for the original photo of the two women by the creek and take it to the police station.

Harry was appalled. It would never have occurred to him that one of the women in the picturesque scene might be a killer! Of course, he had heard about Lesley, but he had no idea that her body had been found right there! In that same location where he had seen the two ladies, apparently painting in peace and harmony. Unfortunately, he couldn't remember much at all anymore. His recollection of dates seemed to get worse after his dear wife had passed away.

And now this photo would serve as evidence in a murder case? But even if he had taken it on the same day of the homicide, it was possible that Mrs. Jane had gone home earlier and Lesley had been killed by someone else later. Or perhaps Lesley had returned to this location at the creek by herself on another day, maybe to finish her painting. Regardless, Harry realized that he had to inform the police as soon as possible. And he hoped they would interrogate Mrs. Jane!

Chapter 16

Sebastian hoped that Mrs. Jane had been arrested by now. But when he arrived at school on Monday morning, she was already sitting at her desk, looking as arrogant as ever. He was shocked! Why wasn't she in prison? And today he had both English and History classes with her, what a bummer! To his further dismay, Mrs. Jane asked him to read a long paragraph, and he had difficulty pronouncing an English word. And once again, she corrected him in a derogatory manner. Later on, in History class, Mrs. Jane looked at a female student with unconcealed contempt as that girl could neither remember the date of a certain battle nor did she know the name of some king. Both that pupil and Sebastian were glad to finish their school day after that class, and yet very disappointed that Mrs. Jane was not in jail. Was she innocent after all? Or was Harry's photo not proof enough?

Everything changed by the next week, though. While everyone else was still eating breakfast, Andy was reading the newspaper, waiting for his second coffee to cool down a bit.

Suddenly he called out: 'Oh no!'

'What happened?' Lizzie asked, alarmed by his tone.

'There was an accident in our town!' Andy replied.

He read the article again, this time aloud. Over the weekend, a young man was driving around too fast, with three drunk youths as passengers, when he caused a bad accident around midnight. The man behind the wheel, who had just gotten his driver's license, had lost control of the car. An 18-year-old pedestrian, on his way home with his girlfriend, was hit by the car and thrown several meters through the air. The girlfriend was unharmed, and she immediately called an ambulance, which arrived a few minutes later. However, the young man is in a critical condition, and it's not certain whether he will survive.

Andy took a sip from his mug and continued reading.

'He is in hospital with severe head wounds and internal injuries and has not yet woken up from his coma.' Then he looked at his family and said, 'His name is Philip Anderson!'

Anna, Sebastian and their mother all started talking at the same time, but Andy interrupted them.

'Wait until you hear the rest, that's not all! Listen! ... The injured man's mother, Mrs. Jane Punch, a teacher at the local school, suffered a complete breakdown at the sight of her son. Due to her hysterical screaming, crying and ranting, she had to be sedated by the doctors at the hospital. As a precaution, she remained there a bit longer for observation. For a while she was silent, but then she started to utter incoherent, confused sentences. When a nurse kept hearing 'sleeping pills', 'poison' and 'killing' over and over again from her mostly unintelligible mumbling, she reported this to the doctors, and the police was alerted.'

Andy cleared his throat briefly.

'Mrs. Jane later made a full confession. She killed a woman at Stumers Creek a few months ago, a young widow named Lesley Williams!'

'We knew it!' shouted Anna and Sebastian.

Their father frowned, but read on. At the same time, he recounted to them in his own words what had supposedly happened.

'Mrs. Jane, as she was usually called, had met the future victim in a painting class. Lesley, who had lost her husband in a tragic accident several years earlier, suffered from depression. She lived a quiet, withdrawn life. However, she started a romantic relationship with her art teacher, Jeremy, who was completely infatuated with her. Unfortunately, Mrs. Jane fell in love with the same man. She thought about how she could win him over and came up with a dreadful idea...'

Andy paused for a moment. Then he continued on,

'Mrs. Jane had once seen a pretty drawing by Lesley and asked her what kind of plant it was. When she learned that the painting depicted the flower of a Datura plant, she read more about this poisonous Angel's trumpet, and a horrific plan began to take shape. She befriended Lesley and eventually suggested that they should paint a landscape at Stumers Creek together. She pretended to be too scared to sit alone in the woods. To avoid being seen by anybody else, she picked out a secluded place that could only be reached on a narrow path, and one that was only known by very few locals. So, one day they met very early in the morning and walked together to the location that Mrs. Jane had chosen in advance. Then they both began to paint the bush scene at the creek.

Mrs. Jane had previously read that a tea made with seeds of the Datura plant could cause not just hallucinations, but also very dangerous intoxication, and even death. Earlier at home, she had prepared a toxic herbal tea that she brought along in a thermos flask. Since the mornings were still very cool in August, Lesley happily accepted a cup of tea. For herself, Mrs. Jane poured a non-toxic tea from another bottle, claiming that it was a special blend of herbs for mild gastrointestinal upset, which would taste rather disgusting.

She hoped that Lesley would not be suspicious and not put off by the taste of her toxic drink! But Lesley only commented that the tea had a spicy flavor. They continued painting for a while, until Lesley was feeling a bit dizzy and nauseous. Jokingly, she said that she had probably already been infected by Mrs. Jane's gastrointestinal trouble. Shortly thereafter, she began to complain of strong heart palpitations and cramps. Her face, which had previously been cheerful, now took on a worried and painfully distorted expression. Suddenly, however, she burst out laughing and wondered why the sky was no longer blue but green. The next moment she became frightened and thought she saw a huge wild animal on the other side of the creek, staring at her with threatening eyes, and breathing fire.

At that time Mrs. Jane also began to get scared. What if Lesley didn't die from the plant poison at all, but went completely nuts? Maybe she would attack her? When Lesley complained that her mouth was very dry, Mrs. Jane quickly poured her another cup of herbal tea, secretly adding a lot of sleeping pills. She had taken them with her as a precaution, because she wasn't certain what effect the Datura poison would have on Lesley.'

'How evil!' Sebastian called out.

Andy nodded gravely and read on.

'Once Lesley was dead, Mrs. Jane dug a shallow hole using a small garden shovel and dragged the body into it. Then she shoveled the loose earth over her victim and placed a few branches on top. She carefully collected all of the art supplies and later burned the paintings. Due to the heavy rainfall over the next few days and the rising water level of Stumers Creek, any remaining traces were soon gone.'

'But why didn't she just give her the sleeping pills from the start? Wouldn't that have been enough to kill her?' Anna asked.

Her heart was filled with horror, remembering the foot in the mud.

Andy read the last section of the long newspaper article before he answered.

'It seems Mrs. Jane wanted to cast suspicion on some teenagers who apparently were already known in certain circles for experimenting with drugs. Allegedly, she has not yet revealed where she got the plant seeds from.'

'Or the police want to keep that information from the public,' Lizzie reasoned.

'Maybe Phil had something to do with that?' Anna suggested.

'And who stole Lesley's shoes?' Sebastian asked.

They all felt sick to the stomach. How could anybody be so brutal?

'So, what's going on with Jeremy now, the painting teacher?' Lizzie asked her husband a few days later.

The news had spread quickly throughout the town, and Andy had got some further information from his customers.

'After Lesley's death, Mrs. Jane made her move on Jeremy. At first, he was devastated by the loss of Lesley, but after a while he fell for her charm and beauty. She herself confessed that she had never been so happy with anyone and that he had often made her laugh.'

'Well, she doesn't have much to laugh about now,' Anna declared, looking grim.

'Why wouldn't Jeremy report Lesley as missing, if they were a couple?' asked Lizzie.

Her husband replied:

'He was at an art show in another country at the time, planning to call her after his return. Since she'd been leading a somewhat solitary life, no one else had noticed that she'd disappeared. She had only worked part-time as a saleswoman, so Mrs. Jane had chosen the perfect time to murder her. When Jeremy received news of Lesley's death, he was beside himself! He allegedly blamed himself for having traveled without her.'

'He can't have been that distraught considering how quickly he rebounded with Mrs. Jane,' Sebastian said contemptuously.

But his mother disagreed with him.

'When you are experiencing a great loss, you are also very vulnerable and highly emotional, and Mrs. Jane took advantage of that. That's how she managed to get close to Jeremy.'

'By the way, does anybody know whose watch our Susi found, back then at the creek?' Sebastian inquired.

'It was Harry's! When he finally went to the police to show them the photo of the women in the forest, they asked him about the watch band, which he instantly recognized as his own. He said that at the end of his walk that day, he walked barefoot across the creek at a shallow part. Just as he was about to reach the bank, he slipped, grabbing hold of a branch at the last moment. However, his watch popped off and fell into the water. And he couldn't find it anymore, because the ground was very muddy. Since he doesn't read the newspaper every day, he was not aware that he had been so close to the crime scene. Furthermore, the body was only found a few days later, and he didn't really pay much attention to the timing.'

'Was there anything in the newspaper today about Lesley's property?' Anna asked her father.

'Yes!' Andy responded. 'Mrs. Jane admitted that she was not only interested in Jeremy, but also in the large property. She recognized its true value when she found out that an apartment building could be built there, which would generate a lot of rental income. She was able to persuade her ex-husband, Phil's father, to participate financially in the purchase of the property and the construction of the new building. She wanted to give her only son a good start in life!'

'Yeah, well, and now Phil is lying in the hospital in critical condition,' said Sebastian.

'What a dreadful story!' Lizzie sighed, and Susi trotted to her and sat down next to her, putting her head on her knee.

Epilogue

Phil had to stay in hospital for many weeks, but eventually he made a full recovery. He was absolutely devastated that his beautiful mother, whom he had always idolized, had turned out to be a killer. He claimed not to know anything about plant poisons, insisting that he had never heard of 'Datura' and 'Angel's trumpet' before. For a long time, Jeremy suffered from the shock that, of all people, his girlfriend Jane had killed his previous beloved friend Lesley! It was impossible for him to believe that Jane had plotted and carried out such a diabolical plan. And he was extremely annoyed that he had fallen for her, having found her first hug so comforting!

Mrs. Jane Punch was arrested and sentenced to life in prison. The locals were relieved that the murder case had finally been solved. Fairly soon, everything went back to normal in the typically quiet, sleepy town. Many students, and especially Sebastian, were happy when they got a new, very nice teacher.

Julie and Kevin, the divorced parents of Barbara, Tom and Lisa, spent more and more time together without having any arguments. Anna couldn't wait to see Scott again. She would meet him in Coolum Beach next week! And Susi and her new friend from the 'Moist Nose Rescue' happily ran around on the beach, even if the sky sometimes looked ominous.

The book 'Deadly Datura' is a work of fiction. Most of the places described in the book, such as Coolum Beach and Tickle Park, actually do exist, but the 'Frogmouth Street' was the product of my imagination.

I also invented the 'Moist Nose Rescue Organization'. However, I used to be a volunteer member of the 4 Paws animal rescue organization ('4pawsanimalrescue') on the Sunshine Coast for several years. In that time, my husband and I took care of many foster dogs until they were successfully re-homed.

The Sunshine Coast Wildflower Festival is a real annual event and a fantastic opportunity to study the local plants. I have attended many of those well-organized walks and nobody ever got lost! The description of the botanical garden and the sculptures is based on my own visits to the beautiful Maroochy Regional Bushland Botanic Gardens in Tanawha on the Sunshine Coast, about 90 km north of Brisbane.

Other crime novels by Marion Birkenbeil

Der Mann mit den gelben Turnschuhen

ISBN 9783750413825 & ISBN 9783750474970

BoD Germany. Language: German

Another story of the German Kuhlmann family in Australia:

A small dog doesn't really enjoy an unexpected white water rafting tour. A bigger dog called Susi is terrified of the skydivers that keep landing on its favorite beach in Coolum Beach, a coastal town in Australia. Sixteen-year-old Anna is suffering from heartbreak, while her thirteen-year-old brother Sebastian falls in love for the first time. Their emotions run high when they find a dead body. What a gruesome discovery! And it turns out that the boy was killed!
The victim was a seventeen-year-old vegan who was committed to animal and environmental protection. Why was he murdered? And why did he have a flipper on his foot? Sebastian and Anna are keen to solve the murder together with their friends. But soon the whole Kuhlmann family gets into dangerous situations, meeting some sinister people and unusual animals ...

A crime mystery for dog lovers from 15 years onwards.

No Fun

An Australian crime mystery (for readers from 15 years onwards)

To be published in the year 2024 / as a translated, reduced and amended version of the original German book as shown above.

Bra over Jumper – My Mum has Alzheimer's

An Australian crime novel from the Sunshine Coast

(for mature readers)

ISBN 978-0-6459818-0-3 (Paperback) and
ISBN 978-0-6459818-1-0 (EPUB)

Published in November 2023. IngramSpark. Language: English.

Michael, 47 years of age, is living on the Sunshine Coast in Queensland, in a beautiful part of Australia. However, his life is not always cheerful. After fifteen years of marriage, his wife Tina wants to split up and stay in their house. Fortunately, he finds a small rental property and keeps the company of his beloved dog. But he becomes increasingly worried about his mother in Brisbane, since she suffers from Alzheimer's disease. One day she almost starts a kitchen fire by accident. What should he do? He and his brother have to find a solution, and fast!

Just when Michael thinks he has everything under control, a mysterious murder happens nearby. Someone finds a half-naked, lifeless woman in a park in Coolum Beach. Who killed her, and why? Michael is horrified, as Tina is living in this normally peaceful seaside town. It turns out that the murdered woman was a nurse named Maureen. But many months pass by without any hints about the culprit and his motive. Maureen's sister and her parents are inconsolable. Michael and Tina can't forget the gruesome deed either, and Tina is more anxious than ever before. And then an acquaintance of them disappears without a trace. Meanwhile, Michael's mother no longer recognises her own sons ...

Note: The original book called 'BH über dem Pulli' has been published in August 2023. Books on Demand. Language: German.

Marion's bilingual baking book

Bake a Cake – Backe einen Kuchen

ISBN 9783750440937 & ISBN 9783751946940

BoD Germany. Language: German & English

This baking book is a bilingual collection of delicious recipes in both German and English. The author Marion Birkenbeil grew up in Germany and has lived in Australia for many years. In memory of her mother, who always entertained her guests with royal hospitality, Marion now presents some traditional cake recipes handed down by her mother as well as her own favorite recipes. In this book you will find traditional and modern recipes, which are clearly explained and supplemented with photos of Marion's cakes and muffins. In addition to tutorials for widely popular cakes such as apple crumble, cherry pie, cheesecake, chocolate and nut cake, Marion gives you ideas for some nutritious vegan treats. She hopes you too will discover the joy and fulfillment baking can bring to friends and family.

Note: a great baking book for people who like to learn either German or English. Each recipe is shown in English on the left page and in German on the right page.

Also refer to: https://m-birkenbeil-autorin.jimdofree.com

The author and her bilingual baking book

Marion's Cheesecake

1) Mix together:

- 100 g softened butter and 100 g white sugar and 1 egg
- 200g self-raising flour

2) Mix together:

- 1kg Greek yoghurt and 200 g white sugar
- 3 full tablespoons of vanilla custard powder
- 2 full tablespoons of corn flour
- 4 egg yolks and the juice of 1 lemon
- 4 egg whites (whisk until stiff and fold into the mixture)

3) Topping (optional):

- Pineapple pieces from a can (approximately 400g) or other fruit

Preparation: Preheat oven to 190°C conventional (or 175°C fan-forced). Mix the ingredients from step 1 and spoon the dough evenly into the base of a greased springform pan (28cm diameter). Top up with the yoghurt mixture and decorate with pineapple pieces or other fruit. Cover with aluminium foil and bake for 45 minutes. Remove the foil and bake for another 15 minutes or longer if needed. Allow the cake to cool completely in the springform, then cover and refrigerate for several hours or overnight before serving.